Weatherman

Anthony Cropper

route

Anthony Cropper

Anthony Cropper was born in Fleetwood, Lancashire. Amongst other things, he has worked as a musician, milkman and teacher. This is his first novel.

First Published in 2001 by Route
School Lane, Glasshoughton, West Yorks, WF10 4QH
e-mail: books@route-online.com

ISBN: 1 901927 16 4

Cover Design: Jackie Parsons

Support:
Thanks to Keith Jaffrate, Julia Darling, Ian Daley, Daithidh MacEochaidh,
Glynis Charlton, Adrian Tanner, Justin Neal, Julia, Marjorie and Geoff.
Thanks for all the help, advice, encouragement, criticism and close
reading. Thanks also to Jackie for the great cover.

Printed by Cox and Wyman, Reading

A catalogue for this book is available from the British Library

Full details of the Route programme of books
and live events can be found on our website
www.route-online.com

Route is the fiction imprint of YAC, a registered charity No 1007443

Weatherman was created as part of The Opening Line, a writer develop-
ment project run by Yorkshire Art Circus in partnership with the Word
Hoard. The Opening Line was funded by the National Lottery through
the Arts for Everyone scheme.

YAC is supported by
Yorkshire Arts, Wakefield MDC, West Yorkshire Grants

For Julia

Preface

And, one by one, points of light disappear. This dry, brittle night, where silence revolves, now emptied of stars, moon and light, fills slowly with sleep.

I dreamt those words last night. I went to bed thinking whether or not to re-read this book, whether or not to revisit old ground. I woke in a sweat as the sun rose, as light crept in through the curtains and, nervously, I wrote down that sentence. It was the first I'd written in twenty years.

What is there to say? Now, it's the afternoon, late October, and I have the book in front of me. Beautiful white clouds drift by the kitchen window. They're low cumulus clouds. The sun is over to the west, and the right part of the cloud is bathed in silver light. I could quite happily place my pen down and sit and watch all day, but that won't let you know what happened. That won't help me to understand.

So, let me tell you.

I'd been trying for years to invent a machine capable of weather control. I'd run small scale experiments on cloud seeding and wind generation but on the 17th of July 1979 I wheeled out the machine for the first time. It was a huge cumbersome thing of wood and steel. I could go into detail, but that's not why I'm here. That's not why I've returned.

Anyhow, on that day, under a perfect blue sky, high pressure, stable, clear air, I tried the machine for the first time. I turned on the screen and set the controls for generation. What I got though was totally unexpected.

The screen flickered into life and a giant cloud appeared, blunt edged, floating over a razor sharp horizon. I watched for a moment or two in shock as the image increased in intensity. But then it faded and in its place, in the black, empty space, a chalk white moon appeared, doubled in the still waters of the docks. I knocked the side of the screen, clicked the control dial and images and sounds from Goole came flooding in.

I saw people I recognised. I saw Ken and Lucy and Florrie. I picked up images from their past, images from their present. I could see right into their minds. I could see their thoughts, their emotions.

So there I was, out back of Old Goole, out in nowhere; listening, watching and recording like I was a scientist. But I was no scientist. If I was, I'd have known my meddling would have had some impact, but it never crossed my mind till it was too late.

9

That sky I told you about earlier has caught my eye again. It doesn't seem a moment ago since I last looked, yet now it's different. The clouds I saw before have gone. The sun's at a lower angle and the light has changed. The trees sway in the breeze. Now, I have an alternative vantage point. Now, I see things differently. Who knows, I may even see the world more clearly. Perhaps I'm more confused than I ever was.

This then, this is my notebook from the time, from twenty years ago. The story; the scenes, the people and the places, were, quite literally, plucked from the air. The machine I invented, the weather machine, did that. This collection of happenings is just a record of how they were shown to me. This is how they arrived. This is what I wrote.

I still don't fully understand what occurred. I still don't know why I saw what I saw, and heard what I heard. But I'll read through it again. I'll add notes, comments, thoughts - whatever - in an attempt to clarify what happened. But then maybe I don't remember too clearly. I seem to recall having that problem once before.

Alfred de Losinge. October, 2000.

Synoptic Chart 1

At this time of the morning
when it's raining hard
I think about things
like those drops
there, on that glass,
in temporary
fragile
paths

Remote Sensing

There's this small book. It's about two inches square and has a black cover. The cover's textured, like leather, and is well worn. Inside there's a series of simple drawings. It's one of those books where you flip the pages and the image appears to move.

The first drawing is of a rocket on a planet. It's ready for take off. The planet and the rocket are in the bottom left hand corner of the page. At the top right there's a small black dot, like a full stop, only slightly larger.

When you flip the pages the rocket, which looks like a big cigar with fins, starts to shake and a cloud of dust comes from its base. The rocket blasts off and flies upwards as if it's coming out of the page. Then, it makes an arc and heads towards the black spot.

The rocket squeezes itself into the hole and as it disappears there's a small puff of smoke. Then there's just this dot on a page. That's the end.

Forwards then backwards. Flip, flip, flip. Backwards then forwards.

That's the way the story goes.

Precipitation

That afternoon Ken came round and we went out back there playing dominoes. Ken was in that old black suit of his. Poor kid. He's grown a lot in the past ten years.

Go on then, I say. Play it. I know you've got it. You've been looking at them so long you can see straight through them. You may as well not turn them over.

Ken waits a while then lays the double six in the centre of the table. He places the tile in exactly the same spot as he's always placed it. I'm looking at him. I don't know what else to do. We've played dominoes for years, ever since he was a kid. When I saw what happened the only thing I could do was get him to come round for a game. So here we are. We're out in the fields. We're playing.

I lay a six-four and say, I should call you double six. You should have your name put on the back of that one. But he's not responding. He's not taking in what I say. So I look up and say, it's brightening up out that way, but it's like he doesn't want to see any further than his hands. For once he's just focused on the table or on the tiles or something. It's difficult to tell.

After a moment or two I say, I thought it was going to rain earlier. Then I look at him again. Sure, I know what he's like. As I said, I've known him since he was a kid. Today though he looks fragile. Today he's thinking about every move he makes. He's careful, slow, precise. But then, in a moment, his mind's off some place else. I know it.

Jesus, his eyes are real blue, you know. They're more blue than this sky. He looks older, too. He's half my age, but he looks older than just a week or so ago. The skin round his eyes is dry, flaky and cracked. Poor kid.

Ken plays a four-two. He positions it so the edges are directly in line with one another. Then he straightens my tile.

You're always fiddling with them, I say to him. It's the same game if they go in straight lines or if they go in circles. It doesn't matter if they're all crooked. I tell you, it's not going to make you win. There's more chance of it raining frogs than you winning this one. Then I tap a tile on the table and say, this game's mine. I can feel it in my bones. I say that, then I smile, but I don't really feel like smiling.

I play a two-zero and he waits a while then plays a one-blank. Then he looks at me with those big blue eyes of his.

This is me, he says.

There's nothing I can do but look up, beyond him, over into the distance. Out that way the sky's gigantic. It's turned to a kind of metallic grey. It makes the fields look greener. It makes everything look sharper. Over there, behind us, towards the river, you can see Ken's house. It looks like it's rusting. The bricks are red, crumbly, dusty.

You know where we are; we're at this table way out in the fields and we're playing dominoes like we've never played before. From the room at the back of Ken's house you'd be able to see us in the distance but you'd hardly notice us. From a distance we're tiny, insignificant.

Ken shuffles the dominoes round on the table. His hands are big. The dominoes clatter together and the sound is lost in all this empty space.

I'm in the kitchen. The weather forecast is for rain. They say there's a low pressure system coming in from the Atlantic.

A while ago I was watching television and this woman was talking about depressions and isobars and about how closely the lines on those systems were packed together. She was only young and had short hair with blonde streaks. She pointed at the screen behind her and said, close isobars mean the winds are going to be strong. This woman had a big wide smile and white teeth. She looked right at me and didn't speak for a second or two. Then she pressed a gadget in her hand and it showed the isobars moving from west to east. The wedge of weather travelled over the country, over the Pennines and on to Goole.

She turned, watched, then looked back at me and said, the whole system is spiralling anticlockwise, and she did this swirling motion with her left hand. She pressed the gadget again and the screen showed one of those satellite pictures of clouds. The clouds jumped from one place to the next. It was like they couldn't get the sequence right and I wondered if anyone thought clouds really moved like that. I thought maybe someone watching might get the impression that clouds sit still for a while in the sky then jump a few miles. The clouds were deep grey and she said the darkest areas are where the rain is heaviest. That whole mass of grey was almost as big as the country.

Then she said there could be localised flooding, and high winds could cause structural damage. She warned people to take care. The winds will pick up, she said, and they could be gale force by midnight. Then she smiled again. The images behind her faded and left her with a cold, blue outline.

Over that way, in the distance, the sky's dark. Maybe it'll rain later. I don't know. Anyhow, the forecast is for a belt of heavy rain. Think I'll just watch these clouds a while to see if they jump.

Synoptic Chart 2

Standing on the blue bridge that crosses the dike you can see down to the docks. At the centre of the docks there's a group of four silos, all silver. The silos are tall, and are connected at the top by tubes and a walkway. Most of the time the silos are used to store grain, some of which is shipped in from Zlotow, in Poland. Sometimes, the silos look a little like silverfish standing on end.

The other tall things around the docks are the cranes. The cranes all lean at the same angle, and are blue. The silos and the cranes stand out against the dull sky, which is almost always the colour of lead.

If you look closely at the silos you can see they're held together by a series of rivets. The rivets make up a regular pattern on the outside of the metal. It's easy to overlook them when you're standing on the bridge looking over at the docks. The thing is, the docks are full of large objects; ships, warehouses, containers, and your eye seems naturally drawn to them. But when you look close, really close, you can see the smallest thing, you can pick out the smallest detail. The early morning light is best for detail. Then, the rivets stand out on that shiny surface.

I've thought about those rivets, and what they do. Grey, tiny little things they are, holding everything together, punched through and locked tight. Removing one wouldn't make much difference, but take out more, and there comes a point where the whole structure becomes unsafe, unstable. This, of course, is the problem.

Over the other side of the bridge there's a row of terraced houses. They were built around the same time as the docks, over a hundred years ago. They're not bad for their age, but they creak and groan. The ground they're built on has dried out, and a few have subsided, you can tell by following the roof line along the road. Ken's house, the house in which he was born, is on the corner, at the far end of the street. It means he has further to walk to work.

Ken lives alone. He's been alone since his mother died, ten years ago. At night the house is quiet, the street is quiet.

The house is dark, and almost empty of possessions. The front faces north and is always shaded. The back faces south, towards the fields, towards wide, flat open space.

There's no carpet on the floors and when Ken walks it echoes loudly. When he makes coffee in the morning the kettle makes the sound of heavy traffic.

Ken is dusty and has cold, chapped hands. He licks his lips yet they remain dry. He's always thirsty, and always hungry. His hair is silver and brittle. Ken cracks the knuckles and joints in his fingers. His skin is stretched tight on his body, like the skin on a drum, and it's prone to blistering in the sun.

For work he wears a T-shirt, braces, a pair of jeans with rivets on the outside of the leg and steel toe-capped boots. Work makes him smell of wheat and metal so he tries to cover this with aftershave. The aftershave makes him wince and leaves him with a rash on one side of his neck. Round his neck he wears a string of wooden beads that were given to him not so long ago.

There's something repetitive about Ken, something monotonous, like a metronome. He sometimes has difficulty breathing, had asthma when he was young, and occasionally uses an inhaler, especially when under pressure. He sucks in the white dust and gasps.

At home Ken eats from tin cans; beans, soups, pies and tuna fish. The tins are kept in a box next to the cooker. Ken owns one steel pan which he scrubs clean with a brillo pad. He eats from a tin plate, like a Scouts plate, and when he eats, the fork scratches on the surface.

Every morning when he goes to the bathroom there's silverfish round the plug hole. He turns on the tap and washes them down. If they stick he flicks them with his finger.

There's a big difference between weather and climate. Climate's generalised data. It's the stuff that's been collected for thirty years or more. It's averaged data on temperatures, rainfall, sunshine hours and the like. Someone asks you about the weather in Goole in summer and you tell them one thing or another. You don't tell them about the weather, you just tell them what you know about the climate, about what kind of thing to expect when they come to visit. It's all generalised. You know that when they go it might not be like you'd said. You don't even know what it's like now; right now.

The weather though, the weather's what's happening at some specific point in time. You don't look out the window and see climate. You look out and see a sky obscured by clouds. It looks like it might rain. You measure the temperature and it's fourteen degrees Celsius, there's not a breath of wind. That's the weather. That's what's happening. That's outside of this window. The sky's uniform. The trees in the distance are blurred because of the moisture in the air. If the clouds were a fraction lower you wouldn't see the trees at all. If the clouds were lower the horizon would be lost in mist.

It's easy, talking about climate, you don't really need to look at anything. As I said, it's easy.

Aneroid Barometers

Now here's a thing. Water evaporates.

Even a block of ice contains heat energy. At zero degrees it still contains heat energy. When someone tells you that for the first time you think, wow. Not ice. There's no heat in ice. But there is. There's a lot of heat in something that's frozen solid.

At absolute zero, which is minus two hundred and seventy three point one five degrees Celsius, there's supposed to be nothing. Nothing exists at minus two hundred and seventy three degrees Celsius. Now there's an idea. Nothing. That's a space with absolutely nothing inside.

A pool evaporates water, a river evaporates water, an ocean evaporates water. Even on the frozen wastes of Alaska some evaporation still occurs. A tiny molecule escapes its field and rises up into the air as a vapour. From a liquid to a gas. And as it rises it cools. It loses energy. That's the way it goes, generally. As air rises it cools. As a molecule rises it cools. And if it cools far enough it condenses. Then, it becomes a liquid again. Condensation is a gas or a vapour turning back into a liquid. A sweet idea, really. And this, this is the beginning of milky white clouds.

That tiny molecule though needs something to condense around. It needs dust or smoke particles, salt, anything. It needs something. If the air is pure, if there is nothing, then supercooling can occur, and condensation might not occur. But to get a cloud forming we need something in the air; some particles.

We need something.

On a sunny day we sometimes see a single cloud in the sky. A single cloud, motionless, in a sea of blue. Beautiful. But, of course, it's only an illusion. Not the beauty aspect. The colours. The sky is not really blue, and the cloud is not really white. Take a jar up there for a sample. Try to get a jar full of colour. There is no colour. It's an illusion. It's colourless. It's just a trick of light. Somewhere else the sky might be red, or orange, or green, or salmon pink. Somewhere else it might be a rich and heady mix of damson, violet, maroon, and indigo. There's not many colours the sky can't be.

But how come, how come in all that blue, in that sea of blue, in that

19

trick of blue that's not blue, in all that immensity, how come there's just a single little cloud?

Well maybe that cloud is like a magnet, and when all those tiny drops of water evaporate, rise up through the air, cool and condense, well maybe they're drawn to one another like bugs to a light. Maybe that cloud is just a water magnet in the sky.

You know, scientists have tried to create nothing. With all the technology they can muster, with the equipment and brains that have put people on the moon, sunk them to the bottom of the oceans, exploded atoms and cities and peoples lives. With all that technology they still can't create nothing. It's incredible. It's a joke. It's a bloody funny joke. But, of course, for some people, the inability to create nothing is a problem. That's when a nothing becomes a something.

Try creating nothing. A space containing nothing; absolutely nothing. The mother of all vacuums. A vacuum to end all vacuums. A space free from the rest of the universe. A space where absolutely nothing from anywhere can be. A nothing like no nothing you can imagine. Not a jot. An idea-less space, a heat-less space, a dust-less space, a light-less space, a cloud-less space, a history-less space, an everything-less space. A nothing inside of a something.

You see, the thing is, we can't evacuate a space, not totally. They take a box, and try to suck out all its insides. That's what they do, scientists. They try to suck the insides of things. They get the most powerful pumps you can imagine and draw out the air. Then they get the most powerful coolants you can imagine, and take out the heat. They want to get it all out. A box with nothing. An empty box. A soulless box.

What a present that would be. A box that if opened it'd suck you in at the speed of light.

They've been trying for years, you know. Day after day getting it further and further down towards nothing. Minus two hundred and seventy Celsius, minus two hundred and seventy one, then two, then three. Fractionally closer and closer. But they still haven't arrived. Not yet. With all the will in the world they still haven't arrived at a space with nothing inside. Minus two hundred and seventy three point one five degrees Celsius. Nought degrees Kelvin. That's nothing.

They've got close though, real close. They've got to nought point two eight millionths of a degree away. Nought point two eight millionths of a degree away! That's 0.00000028 degrees away from nothing. It's a squidge. But in terms of getting there, they may as well be a million miles away, a billion miles away. It's more difficult than putting a man on the moon. Than exploding the atom. More difficult than, well, anything.

Perhaps it can't be done. Maybe nothing does not, cannot, exist.

They talk about space being a vacuum. A vacuum. I suppose it's how you define it. If it's a space entirely devoid of matter, then space isn't a vacuum, not in the true sense. It still has heat energy, for one thing. So it has something, and a vacuum, really, should have nothing. Space isn't a vacuum. There's no space entirely devoid of matter. Seems like some things are impossible.

You know, the vast majority of clouds in the sky are not rain bearing. Over ninety percent are not rain bearing, they just float along, they just float in and out of existence. Gas liquid, liquid gas, sometimes solid to liquid to gas. They're classified under three different types. There's cumulus; fair weather clouds, stratus; sheet-like clouds, and cirrus; high level clouds.

Cumulus clouds are the ones we get on a summer's day. They're the ones that sit lonesome in the belly of the sky. Stratus clouds are the ones that spread themselves across the sky in a huge chalky mass. They're the ones that give us overcast days, the ones that you think might bring heavy rain. Cirrus clouds are the ones we see high up. They're the ones that look like little wisps in the air. The ones that look like horses' tails, or flicks of paint. Cirrus clouds are frozen. They're composed of ice crystals.

That's the three. Three layers. Low, middle and high. It's a bit generalised, but that's the way of things. As soon as we classify anything it's in danger of becoming a generalisation. Give it a name, then abuse it. But what the hell. Let's generalise.

Ken opens the fridge and feels a blast of cold air. He takes out the tin of condensed milk and studies the label. He holds it up, close to his face and reads; slowly, clearly.

Carnation Condensed Milk.

He tilts his head and drops some sweet white liquid into his mouth. He moves it from cheek to cheek, then swallows.

Ken has the can in his hand as he looks into the empty fridge. It's a cold, empty space with nothing inside. He stares, blinks, then closes the door. He lifts his mug from the draining board, moves to the table, sits and sips his tea. It's early morning. Outside it's grey and overcast. He thinks it's probably going to rain.

You know, I see him, now and again, and it's like I'm seeing him for the first time. I just want to walk over to him and take hold of him. I want to lift him down from up there and set his feet on the ground again. Maybe it's thirty or more years ago since we first met. Seems just like yesterday.

Ken used to get all his clothes from his cousin, Ray. They were all hand-me-downs. Ray was a few years older, but saying that, Ken still had trousers up above his ankles and shoes that'd split on the sides. Poor kid. The only thing he ever got new when he was young was a parka. That's how we met. That's the reason we got to know each other.

I remember it was winter and that wind was blowing down from the north. It'd frozen the pipes in my workshop and I'd walked to Old Goole to get some tea and biscuits. I was on the way to the shop when I saw this kid on the school wall. He was real stiff, like a statue or something. I thought he had his back to me but when I got up close I realised his coat was on back to front. It'd been zipped right up and all the strings were pulled in tight. The hood was up and the poor kid couldn't see. His arms were inside the coat and the sleeves were tied together. The playground was empty, all the other kids had gone inside. You could see them at the upper window looking down at him, pointing and laughing.

The first day he'd worn anything brand new in his life and they'd done that to him. I wouldn't mind but he was bigger than all the other kids in the school, even the ones who were two or three years above him. He wouldn't harm a fly would Ken. He'd just take it in and store it up somewhere.

So I said, it's all right lad. I'll get you down.

He was taking long breaths and you could see the back of the hood moving in and out. I climbed up on the wall next to him, undid the arms and the string pulls, then unzipped the coat. I'd never seen him before. Don't know how I'd missed him in such a small place. He had an old face and these eyes that stared out that way, beyond the yard, out to the fields. I was talking to him, saying things like, don't worry, you'll be all right in a minute, but I didn't know if he could hear me. I had to lower him down to the ground like he was a board or something. Stiff with shock, he was. Poor kid.

I said, you're all right now. You're down. But his gaze didn't shift from out that way. I turned and looked to see if there was something there, but there wasn't, not that I could see. It was just some long white cloud over on the horizon.

I thought that'd be the last I'd see of him, but a couple of days later I came out *the workshop and he was there at the gate. He had a box of dominoes in his hand.*

Come on then lad, I said. Let's give you a game then.

Seems like every time we played we got further and further out into those fields. Now we're just a couple of dots in space.

Climatic Data

Today is today, is today, is today. There's no real separation when you think about it. It's not like one thing ends and another begins. This is all today. It's just an expression. It's just a way of categorising things. It's just a way of giving things some order.

This is full of todays, but don't let it worry you. It's a whole load of todays stacked together, one on top of the other. Just think of it like it's all happening at once. Just think of it like it's a today from last year, a today from last month, a today from last week. Flick through it. Fan your face with a year or so. Pick up on some of the names of the people and places. It only takes a second or two. Today is today is today. See them all flip by. It's not like they're separated at all. It's not like there's hours, days and months and years between them. They're close. They're so close you could take them out and shuffle them round and it wouldn't make much difference.

It's late and I look out of the window. It's Autumn and the sun's almost gone. The light bulb's reflected in the glass. A single bulb on the end of a wire. I can see the shelves, the table, and I can see myself. I'm watching my hands as I write. I'm alone in this old house.

The day's disappeared quickly. It was hot, dusty, fine for the time of year. I can't help thinking that this is the last of the good weather. Sure, there might be the odd warm day to come, but this last week's been dry. The ground's baked hard. Something has to change soon, and once it does, then that'll be it till next spring.

Out of this bedroom window the sky's thick and grey. There's a few speckles of rain on the glass. The rain's getting heavier, but over in the distance the sky's bright. Miles away, over there, there's a yellow band of light low down in the sky. Over there it's like the world's floodlit. It's like it's getting ready for a show.

I've been having dreams about Ken and Lucy. I don't think it's right. It can't be good for me to be still dreaming about the two of them. I got up in the middle of the night and put the small light on. I looked at myself in the dressing table mirror and told myself to stop dreaming. You're an old man, I said. Just look at you. You have to stop all this dreaming. Leave these people alone. Let it rest, I said. But then maybe it was all my fault.

I got back in bed, lay down and closed my eyes. I saw Ken and Lucy. They were together and they had their backs to me. I shouted but they didn't move. They were staring at something, but their backs were in the way so I couldn't see what it was. They held hands and were silhouetted against a yellow sky. Ken's way, way taller than Lucy. I cupped my hands round my mouth and shouted, Lucy. Lucy. But she was just a black figure in front of me. It's like I was talking to the night. There wasn't even an echo. I wanted the wind to blow hard or something so they'd be blown over. But there was no wind. There's not been a breath of wind for a while now.

I painted a picture of them when I woke up. I didn't have breakfast. I've not eaten breakfast for weeks now. I got out of bed, and in my night-shirt went straight into the back room and painted a picture of the two of them. They were like trees; like sad trees. It was like a picture a kid would paint. They were just simple lines. I didn't even know they were Ken and Lucy till after I'd done them. I was just painting. I did one, then the other, and when I looked I saw I'd painted the two of them. Two solid lines for Ken. Two dead thin ones for Lucy. The sky was slate grey and the ground blood red. Ken and Lucy. On top of everything. On top of the landscape. Up on the roof of some flat, featureless world.

The two of them stood out sharp, like they were about to fall off the canvas, like they were about to leave the picture. I'd painted their arms by their sides but when I looked again their arms were above their heads. They reached up like they were trying to grasp hold of something. But then they were both still and the sky was still.

It was afternoon by the time I'd finished. I stared at the picture awhile then went and made some toast. I sat in the kitchen and ate. Crumbs dropped on the Formica table and when I'd finished I swept them into a small pile. I looked up and Lucy was opposite me. She smiled and when she smiled I saw she had sunken eyes and yellow teeth.

Soon be dead, she said and she laughed like a little girl.

Isolines

You get maps and charts for all sorts of things. I've got some soil maps, some geology maps. I've got a map of the sea floor and a map of waterways. I've got a map that shows the comings and goings of mackerel and plaice. I've got a map of heights round here, and a map showing where people live. I've got a map of the climate that shows rainfall, temperatures and wind speed and things. I've got all of that, but I tell you, I haven't got a map or chart of the sky. Sure, there's maps of stars and planets, but I haven't seen a cloud map, not yet, anyhow.

You see, maps are just generalisations. They're just pictures. They're metaphors. They're abstractions. They don't tell you what's really going on. Not really.

Partially Evacuated Boxes

Ken licks his lips, opens his eyes and sits up. The blankets drop from his chest and he looks directly ahead. He blinks, sighs, then pulls the curtains to one side. It's early morning. Out the front of the house he can see over to the docks. The docks are still and quiet.

The sky behind the docks is purple, almost black. From the window you can just about see the river. Some small spots of silver flicker on the surface. That's north, out front. That's the view to the docks, the river, the silos, the cranes and the bridge. He raises a hand to his mouth and touches his lips. His lips are dry, like the skin around his eyes.

There's a store for grain that's standing on the edge of the dock. It's close to the water so the contents can be moved quick and easy. It's near the water but it's a store that's bone dry. Inside, there's not a drop of moisture in the air.

I could tell you about the ground the silo stands on, about what it looks like from various angles. But you get the picture. It's a silo. It's tall and not so wide. It's just a store, that's all. It's a piece of industrial equipment that's there for a specific purpose. It's a container with a thin shell. It's something that's been hammered and riveted into shape. It's something that's been coated in paint, then left to weather in the elements. It's a silo.

Most of the time the silo's silent. Stand next to it in the middle of the night and it won't disturb you. Put your hand on its rippled surface and all you feel is the chill that's built up there since the sun went down. That's what it's like in the middle of the night on the docks in Goole. I know. I've been there.

Ken releases the curtain, lays down and he stares up at the ceiling. There's a musty smell in the air, like old wood, like dusty carpets.

There's no time any more, he thinks. Everything's gone. Everything's empty and this is everything. That's what he thinks as he stares into near empty space.

At night the ground round here's blacker than the sky. It's like you're at sea. You can see a few tiny lights in the distance. You can see an orange glow that might be a town or a city. But you're at sea. The lights stay in the distance. There's a world of things over this way, and that. You lean back and look up at the stars. You wonder if the moon will appear. You wonder if there's anyone up there in that blackness looking down at you. You close your eyes and breathe in the cold flat air.

Sun Spots

Ray has a magnifying glass he got for his birthday. It's only a cheap little thing in a red plastic pouch but Ken's still got the mark on his arm. A big round spot like a cigar burn.

They're in the garden:

Look at this, says Ray. You focus it down like this.

Ray moves the magnifying glass close to the cardboard.

See the sun? he says. You need to get it just there, where it's a tiny white dot. The smaller you get it, the stronger it burns. See?

He moves the glass forwards and backwards and when the sun's a sharp dot he holds it in place. A second or two later and a thin stream of smoke rises from the card. The sun spot turns brown then black. Then there's the smell of burning in the air.

See, says Ray. It's magic. I've got the sun in my hand, he says.

He drops the card onto the floor. It burns in front of them.

Look, says Ray. I've written my name on the side of my shoe.

He holds up his shoe and on the plastic heel RAY is written in joined up burn holes.

He puts his shoe back on then rolls up his sleeve.

Watch this, Ken. I can hold it on my arm for three seconds. He moves the magnifying glass forwards and backwards until there's a small sun on his forearm.

One, two-three, he says. Wow that burns. Gleddy says he can do it for five seconds but I don't believe him, he's always lying.

Ray looks at Ken. The two of them are almost the same size. Ray's eleven. Ken's seven.

Let's see how long you can go, he says.

Ray rolls up Ken's shirt to the elbow.

Here, he says, I'll focus it. You just keep your arm there. Hold still now.

There, he says.

One...two...three...four...

The sun burned bright in a cloudless sky.

31

You see? That was Ken, when he was just a kid. I sat at that machine of mine, watching that. I could see and hear it all as clear as day. I should have switched it off and burnt it there and then, but curiosity got the better of me. So I clicked the cloud dial round another notch and the image on the screen changed to one of Lucy.

Coriolis Force

Lucy. Tall, thin, blonde hair and a suntan. That's me. Florrie calls me Luce, but she's just taking the piss.

She smiles into the mirror.

Abusive, yes, common, yes, flirty, yes, dirty, sometimes. Hard, yes, and tough, yes. You have to be round here, or you'd get eaten alive.

She takes a chain from the jewellery box that's in the centre of the dressing table.

I like yellows, browns and golds. But mustard's my favourite; a mix of all of them. I've got a mustard coloured front door, mustard coloured carpets. I've even got mustard coloured walls in the rooms.

She smiles again, fastens the chain round her wrist then takes a cigarette from the ashtray. She inhales slowly then gradually releases the smoke in the direction of her reflection.

Hides the tobacco stains for one thing.

She brushes two or three flecks of ash from her shoulder.

This is my favourite outfit. White jacket and trousers, high heeled boots, and a leopard skin top.

Lucy pulls up both boobs then rubs her hands down to her waist.

Look at my figure in this. Not bad for someone my age. Still a few years left in me yet. Oh I still get the looks, sure I do. But I know what they're attracted to. You can't kid a kidder.

She pulls her jacket down at the back, then straightens the collar.

I've still got my shape.

She shakes a tube of mascara, pulls out the brush and looks back at her reflection.

I like dark eye make up. The darker the better, I always say.

She laughs.

It's like I never left the sixties. What's her name now? Sandie Shaw. Eyes like Sandie Shaw. I should have had them tattooed, or dyed or something. Christ. The number of years I've spent in front of this mirror getting ready to go out. It frightens me. All that time readying myself for the same old places, the same old people. It's the same today as it was twenty years ago. People still dancing to the same old stuff night after bleeding night.

She closes one eye and runs the mascara brush over the lashes.

My mother said life goes in circles. What goes around comes around, she said. I remember it well. I was young and I wondered what on earth she was talking about. But now I know it's a load of old cod. It's not circles. If it was circles then it wouldn't be speeding up. Life's one of those things that gets faster and faster all the time, like it's out of control. It's a spiral, that's what it is. A spiral getting faster and faster. We see similar situations but they fly past more quickly every time. Familiarity, I suppose. I hate it.

Lucy finishes one eye, then starts the other.

Then we get a new phase now and again. You know, we meet someone new, have a child, a divorce, a death in the family, buy a dog. And we think for a second, for a brief bloody moment that it might change our lives, that it might relieve all the monotony, that things might start to get better. But it doesn't. It ends up reverting back to the same old mess. Who said we're meant to be happy? What a great con. It's like believing in Father Christmas. It's a myth. We tell each other things, spin stories, and because they sound good, we want to believe them. We really want to believe them. But who said it was supposed to be like that? Who said we were meant to be happy people in a happy world? We did, that's who. We said it to each other. My mother told me. School told me. Everyone told me. Believe in true love, believe in happiness, believe, believe, believe. Things will work out, things will get better, you'll be happy in the end. Well it's the myth of Santa. A huge myth we've spun to each other to keep us from going mad. To keep us all from jumping off the nearest roof top. Well I'll tell them what to do with their belief.

She finishes her eyes, replaces the brush then positions the tube near the other make-up.

My lad's left home now. He got an apprenticeship over in Hull. He used to drive at first, but it's a long way, and it's the money as well. You know how it is when you're young, not wanting to be at home with your mother. Now he's moved in with Shirley. Shirley. What a name for an eighteen year old. I expected her to have a bubble perm and a chubby little face. But no. She's posh. Works in the civil service. Got a good job. Anyhow, I just hope things work out for them. Jesus, I wish I could make them know, really know, about some of the mistakes I've made. I don't want them to be like me. You'd think after millions and millions of years of existence, of so called evolution, that we'd have managed to sort something a little better than this. I sometimes think I wouldn't mind going back to the cave.

She looks at her reflection.

Only they wouldn't have mirrors, I suppose.

She stubs out the cigarette and takes another from the box to her left. She holds the cigarette at the tips of her fingers.

At least I don't see the ex anymore. That's a blessing, I can tell you. When he first left he lived just round the corner with that fat tart. God. Every bloody day I had to look at her. She'd glance over at me in the shop, or peer out from behind those stupid net curtains, and she'd have this wry little smile, a little slit of a smile, that said she'd got something I wanted. I told her. I said you can have the bastard. Better off without men, that's what I say. Better off without them.

She sighs deeply.

Mind. I can't say that I don't like attention. Sure. I let them come back here now and again. But it's generally a let down. I have to go round with bleach, get rid of the smell from the toilet, and wash the sheets. They've a funny smell, you know, men. They smell different from women. Florrie can tell if one's been back here. She comes in my room here, sniffs and says, So, you had a bit of joy last night.

She clears her throat.

A bit of joy. That's a funny way of putting it. I don't know if it's a pleasure or not. It's like something builds up inside me. I get desperate, and then when it happens it's all a bit of a washout. Besides, they're usually too drunk to manage.

She takes a tube of lipstick, purses her lips then holds it a fraction away from her mouth. Then she places it down again.

I had one, back here one time, he's never been in the club since. He went and pissed all over my coffee table. I'd gone into the kitchen to make a drink and when I came back he was just standing there, eyes closed, trousers round his ankles. Asleep, he was. Pissing in his sleep. I pushed him over, onto the couch and he came to. Piss all over his trousers, all over the table, over the digestives I'd just put out. He got up and ran out. Never said a word; no goodbye, no thanks for the invite, no nothing. He just pulled up his wet pants and scarpered.

She gazes into the mirror and presses the bright red lipstick onto her lips. She runs it smoothly and evenly from one side to the other. Then she pouts and smacks her lips together. She twists the base of the tube, replaces the lid, then places it down next to the mascara.

Lucy sighs, then lifts up an ornate perfume dispenser from the right side of the dressing table. It has a bright orange cloth ball on a small tube protruding from its top. She sprays her neck then glances back into the mirror.

But that's not the worst. Oh no. That's not the worst by a long chalk.

She looks at the bottle, sprays herself on the other side of her neck, then replaces it on the table top.

I don't even like to think about it. Ugh. Disgusting. I was sick for days.

She pats her hair, pushes up her fringe, wets her thumb and forefinger, then pulls at a thin strand.

We'd had this do at the club. You know, chicken and ribs cooked outside like we're all cavemen. And this guy, Geoff, he came back here with me. Anyhow, we did it. Then, in the middle of the night, I was woken up by the bed bouncing around. I flicked the light on and there he was, jumping up and down, holding his backside. He had the runs like I've never seen runs before. It was like a hose pipe, or some volcano erupting out of him. It squirted all over the place. All over the blankets, onto the carpet. It was even on this mirror here. Ugh! Then the stupid sod jumped off the bed and onto the floor, like he was going running or something, and all the time he was just shouting, It's the chicken, it's the chicken. On the bed, I said to him, for Christ's sake stay on the bed, that's a new carpet. I'll give him chicken, I thought. I'll wring his bloody neck for him if he doesn't get off that carpet.

Anyhow. I sorted it out. Got some more blankets out of the spare room, my lad's old room, and put the others in a bin bag. What a smell.

She sighs.

Then the worst thing. And you won't believe this. After all that cleaning, after changing all the blankets and settling down again; he did it again. An hour later, must have been four in the morning, the stupid sod did it all over again.

Well, I can laugh now. But that's just my luck, that is. That's just my luck. And you know. I thought I wouldn't see him again in the club, either. But he was there all right, the next night, at the bar, laughing and joking with his mates. Never said another word to me he didn't. Not a single soddin word.

She lifts the perfume bottle up again.

I got this perfume just after it'd happened. I went to the chemist's and asked for the strongest smelling stuff they had. I wanted something to cover up the stench. I was having my sister and her husband over the following week, and I didn't want the whole place to smell like no sewer. So I doused the whole house; carpets, curtains, skirting boards; the lot. I don't suppose I need to wear it anymore, but I do. I got that used to the smell I wear it all the time. Eau de Toilette. That's what it is. Eau de Toilette. Eau de Geoff, I call it. Eau de Chicken Geoff. I always cluck when I go past him. Cluck, cluck, cluck, I go. But he never says anything. I wouldn't mind if he'd say sorry. But he just kept going on about the bloody chicken. It's the chicken, it's the chicken, he'd say.

She sighs and gazes down at the collection of make-up.

So I don't trust them anymore. I let them come back here, but tell them they can't stay over.

She lifts a jar of nail varnish.

I like this colour. It glitters. Red with tiny gold flakes. Real gold it says on the label. It matches this necklace, and my earrings. Gold looks good on tanned skin. It's what they wear in Marbella. You don't see anyone wearing silver in Marbella. You can't even get it in the shops. It's all gold, like the sun. Bright gold.

If you can get perfume that overcomes the shitty smells, maybe they should sell something that overcomes shitty memories. But what the hell. We've got to go on. Got to keep going. Onwards and upwards, higher and higher, up to the edge of that precipice.

She finishes her nails then stretches out her hands.

That's it. All done.

She pats her hair and smiles.

Ready again. Tonight's line dancing night down at the club. Me and

Flo are off in half an hour or so. I'll put some music on to get me in the mood. A bit of Tom Jones should get me going. And maybe a glass of Martini. Yeah. What the hell. I might even make it a large one.

I was hooked, you see. I was three or four miles away from her yet I may as well have been sitting in the room whilst she poured out her heart. I saw more than if I was in that damn room with her.

Of course, then, I wanted to follow her. I wanted to see what happened when she went out. I wanted to see who she met. I turned the dial, and the sounds and the pictures just kept coming and coming.

Vapour Trails

There's only three of them. There's only Ken, and Lucy and Florrie. That's only three people. Not many, really.

Ken's a funny one. I like Ken. I thought I wouldn't, you know. When I first saw him I thought he was like some monster. But he's not. He's no monster. No. Ken's out in the fields or on some roof top somewhere. He's staring over to where clouds come from. Look, he says. Can't you see? Then he raises his hand and shades his eyes. Over there, he says.

Poor kid. It's like he responds to the most subtle of changes. It's like he feels the passage of clouds, like he feels pressure changes, like he senses changes in humidity and temperature.

Now Florrie, she can't help the way she is. She just doesn't know what to say. She's in the mud, you see. The mud's like fat stuff, like grease and she's sinking. To her sides are embankments. She's in some channel and she can't escape.

And Lucy? She's burning up. She's burning out, like a cigarette. She's on the pavement and she's staring up at the sky. She's glowing bright red.

Some people thought he was going to jump, you know. But not me. No. He's not going to jump, I said. He could just step off that roof and stride out over the river if he wanted to. He didn't get up there to jump. Not Ken. There's some other reasons why he was up there, but that's what I'm here to tell you about. That's where it's all been leading to. That house. That roof. That view out back. This was all only ever going one place, you could see it a mile off.

I was just thinking, says Ken. I was just thinking about the first time I saw a mountain.

Ken sighs and watches the clouds glide across the horizon. They're low and he shades his eyes.

I wanted to tell him they were just vapour but I couldn't get the words out. I couldn't help but look over at them, too.

I'd seen mountains in books, sure I had, but they were just pictures, they were tiny, on a page. I sat out there and saw these two snowy white clouds and saw Ken's two outstretched grey arms. I don't know. Ken said it was a mountain. There's a mountain, he said. See the snow?

Seems like it's years ago since Lucy stopped laughing. I wanted her to laugh again, you know. I wanted her to smile and poke him and say, don't be daft, they're just clouds. I wanted her to tut like she does. I wanted her to turn away and roll her green eyes. But she couldn't, not Lucy. She couldn't reach him from down there on the floor. Lucy looked up into a pale blue sky and Ken stared down into a deep green sea.

I already told you I'd known Ken since he was a kid. His cousin used to live out that way, near my place. It's funny, really. On the road from Old Goole to Swinefleet there's these farms set back almost a mile from the road. That's where Ray used to live, over beyond the wheat over there. That's where I used to see Ken, all those years ago. He'd be standing there, watching for something or other. I don't know what it was about him, but there was something unusual, something magnetic.

I could tell, sometimes, when we were out there playing dominoes, that he was really miles away. You only had to glance at him to know his mind was off someplace else. I don't know what really went on in that head of his. I still don't know him, even after all this time and a thousand games.

Sometimes we never said a word to each other, you know. But there wasn't a problem with that. I could cope with that. He'd been through a lot, you see.

Visibility

For years I'd wanted to write a book about living in Goole and Swinefleet. But I thought about it for a while and decided against it. Then I had some brain wave and thought I could change the names. Maybe then I could write a book without upsetting anyone. So I changed the names. For Goole read Swinefleet, for Swinefleet read Goole.

So then I thought I could write about Ken. We used to meet up together, you know, to play dominoes. But that was a while back. I don't remember too clearly. It's not like I see him much anymore.

I told him. I said, Ken, I'm thinking of writing a book about life round here, like a local history book or something. He was looking over at the clouds over there, the ones way in the distance. The clouds were small and white and were perfectly still.

He looked down at me and said, if you want to write about anything then write about that. If you don't, then just stand here. He said that, then he turned away. He's taller than me, you see. He can see further. He looks down at the horizon. We stood together for a while and we didn't say another word to each other, not a single one. That's probably the last time I saw him. Poor kid.

It started to rain over there, miles away and I wanted to say something stupid like look at the colour of the sky or something. But I didn't. I just stood there like some dumb kid next to him.

Later, I was out back where I live. The moon was up and I thought it might rain. The moon was small and white and round in the night. I looked at that shiny spot in the darkness and said, all right Ken, I'll do it. But this has to be for you. This is not just about clouds and distance and empty spaces. It's not exactly what I want to say or do, but this is it. This is for you.

So, I went against my word. I did what I said I wouldn't do. I must have lied to myself or something. Maybe I knew all along that I was going to write this. Maybe everything else I did was just preparation. But this, now, this is it. This is the world of Ken. Kenworld. It's about him, about Lucy, and Florrie, and about a whole mass of other things.

They fall in love, you know. It's so unlikely you won't believe it. But sure, that's what happens. Ken falls in love with Lucy. Florrie's already in

43

love with Lucy. And Lucy? She can't help but fall in love.

But then poor Florrie tries to stop it all. She doesn't want to be on her own. She doesn't want Lucy to leave and go over the bridge. But then someone dies and everything gets blamed on a pair of muddy brown boots. A pity, really. It's a pity how things work out sometimes. This is just a love story, I suppose. I just wish I could tell you a different one, but this is the only one I have.

So there you go. I'll tell you about it and you can make up your mind. You can read this and think, so what? Nothing's really happened. A couple of days went by, some people met, fell out, did things they regret. You can say to yourself, I don't believe a word. There's no such place as Goole or Swinefleet. There's no place that's as flat as that. There's no place with a sky like that. I don't know these people, so what does it matter? No, you say. It's just words on a page and I can close the book and put the book down some place. Then you can let the memory of this slip from you just as simply as a stone slips off a roof. But me? I can't forget that easily. All I have to do is look out the window. All I have to do is look out across the rooftops to the fields and to the horizon to be reminded.

This is just a story. That's all. It's a damn short story, and I guess it doesn't seem like much, but what the hell. Nothing seems like much from a distance.

I've spent a year or more trying to describe what it's like round here. I built up this stockpile of images and metaphors and things, then put them all together and wondered how accurate it all was. It's like some huge jigsaw. Maybe it's a bit disjointed. Maybe it's a bit confused and contradictory. Maybe I repeat myself and say things that aren't true. But life's like that. I'm like that. I tell lies. I can't stop myself. I make things up. I deceive people. I invent things. But then how else can I make sense out of the world. That's what I do. That's what we all do. We're all inventors, come to think of it. I'm an inventor, that's all. Inventing stories and people and places. Sure, I do it every day.

I had this dream last night. I was in a car with my mother and father. It was only a small car and I was in the back. My father was in the driver's seat, though he doesn't drive, and my mother was next to him.

My mother looked by far the worse of the two. She had cancer, and was almost bald. Only a few strands of hair remained at the side of her head and she had a purple mark just above her ear. She smelled of rotting meat, like a bag of bones, and she kept straining round to look at me.

Soon be dead, she'd say cheerfully.

Then she'd raise a hand and pat down her hair with her stiff fingers. The passenger side window was open and I could feel the air on my face. I wanted to open it wider to overcome the smell, but I knew it would only blow her hair.

My father was wearing a brown-green suit. The suit was tight on his body and was old, though it'd hardly been worn. He had a flat cap made of the same material and it was pulled down, fast on his head. He said he wanted to walk up Slater Place. Slater Place was the steepest hill round where we lived, though it wasn't that steep. It just seemed so when I was young.

With any luck the walk might give me a heart attack, he said. He got out and the car shook. Then he leaned in through the window.

Here you are, he said. I've got something for you.

He took some slips of paper from his side pocket and held them out for me. They were his Premium Bonds, just three or four of them, a few pounds worth.

No, Dad, I said. You keep them. You might win. Or I'll give you the money for them, then you can spend it.

But I'll be dead this afternoon, he said.

He looked surprised, as if I didn't understand.

A walk up Slater's should kill me off, he said.

My mother turned round again. Her false teeth were yellow.

Go on, ave em, luv, she said. He wants you to ave em. Go on, she said.

I took the Premium Bonds and watched my father start off towards the hill. His shoulders rolled like John Wayne's as he walked. He looked fit, fit for his age. I knew he wasn't going to die.

The next thing was we were at the top of the hill, still in the car. The car was cramped like a mini but was older, more old fashioned. My father walked up the hill towards us. He walked quickly and smoked a roll-up.

I thought of him when he'd just come home from the war. I wondered what he must have been like, a twenty four year old that had just spent four years fighting,

45

returning home to marry my mother.

I don't want to take these, I said.

My mother looked round at me. Her eyes were sunken into little hollows. Her skin was yellow-white.

You tek em, luv, she said. You tek em.

Her head was twisted round so she could see me. The skin on her neck was creased and folded.

I looked at her left arm. It was swollen up with the cancer. She could only move two of her fingers. Her index finger curled as she spoke. Then she smiled a big smile.

Soon be dead, she said again.

She chuckled and the car rocked from side to side.

Stability

In the morning Ken usually sits on the end of the bed and pulls on his
black jeans. That's normally what happens. But today things are different. Today he's in front of the open wardrobe. On the rail there's a
leather belt and the black suit he bought for his mother's funeral. That
was almost ten years ago. On this morning he takes out the suit and lays
it on the edge of the bed. He removes the plastic wrapping then holds
the suit in front of him. He stares for a moment then picks a small piece
of white cotton from the lapel. The cotton falls to the floor.

I'd like to say the cotton falls slowly, but it doesn't. It falls as fast as a
stone. Maybe the air's been taken out of the room and there's no friction. If there was friction, or resistance, or a draught or something then
maybe it wouldn't fall so fast. It doesn't twist or curve in the air, no. It
drops quickly onto the hard surface without a sound.

Ken stares down at his feet.

Weather Records

Are they your gardening shoes, eh Brissy?

It's his cousin's feet, Ray's feet. Ray's smiling, and laughing.

Ken. Come and look what I got.

Brissy, Brissy, Brissy. They your gardening shoes, eh Brissy?

He's in the yard, out in the yard.

I'll make a pot, he says. It's nearly eight, she'll be wanting a cup of tea. I'll make a pot.

Grey and green check trousers and a brown shirt. Do your button up, then. You can't go to a funeral with your top button undone.

It's all right. Don't worry. It's all right.

The rocket's ready for lift-off. Three, two, one. Flip, flip, flip.

Crack.

It's a fat cigar with fins on.

Three, two, one; lift-off.

Brissy, Brissy. Cat died, eh Brissy?

See the rocket disappear. Watch it go into the hole.

Look though the magnifying glass. Does it hurt yet?

The chisel hits the rock and sends splinters into the air. Electricity in the air. It's all tiny pieces. It's made up of tiny, little pieces.

I'm frightened of the air, says Lucy.

Lucy. Don't look down. Get down Lucy. You'll fall.

Move your hand, squeeze. Hold on to me, that's right.

See the blue sky.

That sun's blistering.

That's it. It's focused there. Don't move now and I'll count. One...two... Hold still now.

I was driving home the other night and was looking over at some clouds in the distance. There was only a couple of them, but they looked as big as mountains. They had flat bases, and steep sides. The bases went on and on, stretching out across the distance, just above the horizon. It made me think about them coming unstuck and floating up into the air. Then I thought maybe that's what happened after all. Maybe the hills came unstuck round here. Maybe Ken and Lucy and Florrie just unhooked themselves and floated off into space.

Ken never talked that much to me, you know. I knew some things about him, but they were just the bits and pieces I'd picked up from the talk in town. He never told me anything about his family. I never asked. So when I saw things like that, things about when he was a kid, it drew me in further.

I could see him forming in front of my eyes.

Lapse rates

Ken's staring out of the window. It's been a strange kind of a day. It started off fresh and bright, then it turned windy, then it poured for an hour or more. Now it's calm and quiet.

Over in the distance, beyond the fields, beyond the line of trees, there's a bank of bright silver clouds in a vast blue sky.

Ken's in the kitchen. It's silent. That's a little unusual for this time of the morning. Usually there's noise from passing traffic. But today there's no noise. Today it's quiet.

The kitchen is old, like the rest of the house. The pipes over at the sink are lead. They run along the brickwork then down under the floor. They're grey, cold and dry.

Ken's at the table. He's looking out of the window and he's drinking a cup of hot, sweet tea. It's strong tea. It's tea in a cracked cup. It's cheap tea. It's tea with the tea bag still in. It's hot sweet tea made with Carnation Condensed Milk. He's wearing a black suit and he's staring out of the window. The window faces south.

You can't see much besides the sky from this window. Maybe that's one reason why he's watched the sky for so long. Maybe that's why he knows so much about clouds. He grew up staring at clouds. He doesn't know to call them cumulus or nimbus or cirrostratus. He doesn't know the classifications, the generalisations, but he knows which bring rain and which bring snow. He knows them by their shadows. He knows them by the shapes they make in the sky, by the speed they move. He's always watched them. He's watching them now as he drinks his tea.

Ken doesn't feel the heat of the cup. He doesn't feel its heat when he drinks the near boiling liquid. He just sits in the kitchen, stares out of the window and he drinks. He drinks the bronze coloured tea until the cup is bone dry. The tea leaves him with a dusty taste in his throat, like he's still thirsty, like he wants more, like he needs something else.

Ken doesn't walk anywhere, you know. No. He jumps from one place to another. He's been all round here, all over the fields and the farms, but he can't remember getting to them. He doesn't remember the journey. He remembers standing in a field of wheat or grass. Sure, that's all clear to him. He remembers the view out the back. He remembers the sky. That's all there, all at the front of his mind. But he doesn't remember the walking. He doesn't remember the getting there.

I found out the other day how much a cloud weighs. I couldn't believe it. If you were there I would've asked you to guess. If Ken was there I'd have asked him. But you know what he's like. He probably already knows stuff like that.

I did ask some people I knew though. One of those cumulus clouds, I said. You know, the ones you see in summer. The low ones. The ones that look like sheep or puffs of smoke or something.

They thought it was a trick question. So I told them how big a typical cloud was. I said, on average, a cumulus cloud's about a kilometre, by a kilometre, by a kilometre. That's like having some huge box full of a cloud, I said. Then they looked at me awhile. So I told them they could tell me in pounds or even in bags of sugar if they wanted.

It doesn't weigh anything, said one of them. Then they nodded in agreement and laughed. But it does, I said. It's no trick. How much does it weigh? So another said something like twenty pounds, or half a tonne or something.

On average, a cumulus cloud weighs about one and a half billion pounds. That's about a million tonnes. Or, if you want to think of it another way, it's about seven hundred and fifty million bags of sugar stuck up there in the air.

When you say that you see them look up at the sky and think but how do you weigh it? You can see them churn it over and over. Then they're thinking about all that weight up there, wondering where the trick is.

Then someone says, so how come it doesn't fall out of the sky? If it weighs a million tonnes then why doesn't it fall down? And they imagine a solid lump of cloud a kilometre by a kilometre by a kilometre falling out of the sky and crashing to the ground like some huge great sugar cube.

Why do you think? I say. Then they look out of the window again, and I watch them think about the clouds there, in the sky.

Then someone says, it's the wind. The wind keeps them up. Or, it's because they're spread out, or it's because they're gas, or there's no gravity, or someone's holding them up, or they're not really a million tonnes after all. That's what they say, sometimes.

Frontogenesis

Ken's there, opposite me. You know, when I look at him I see the weather. I see brilliant sunshine and blue skies. Then I look away for a second or two and when I look back he's grey and overcast. That's Ken. He changes by the second. That's what I see when I look at him. But the people over that way, over the bridge, the people in those houses, over that side of town, they're not seeing the weather at all. They're looking out their windows and they're seeing the climate. They're seeing average rainfalls, hours of sunshine and prevailing wind directions. They're seeing thirty years of generalisations. But there, opposite me, on that stool, is Ken. He's got a hand full of domino tiles and he's staring at the table. I just wish I could tell you more about the weather. I just wish I could show you what he's like. Poor kid. Seems like he was born for this game.

I'd said to him, Ken, there's a do on at the club tonight, but I didn't think he'd be interested. He's never been interested before. It's some line dancing do, I said.

He's hardly been over that old bridge but I said I'd meet him. I'll see you there at eight, I said. I'll be at the bar. Come out for a change, you never know, you might like it. You don't have to dance or anything. I don't dance. I just go to watch. We'll have a beer and a laugh. Sure, that's what we'll do.

Then I made him promise he'd come. He nodded to me when I asked him again. Are you sure you're going to come? You promise? He looked at me and nodded. But I never made it. I made those arrangements and never arrived. I told him I'd twisted on my ankle on the stairs just before going out. Poor kid. I left him to those climatologists over that way.

So, he's at the bar. He's standing there, looking round for me, but I'm not there. I'm out in these fields; watching, listening. I've got my hand on this dial and I'm thinking about Ken.

Ken looks at the palms of his hands, then over into the distance. The clouds have thinned and the sky's turned light grey. See, he says. See what happens? I'm just going to stand here, he says. No one can see me. No one knows I'm here, he says.

Visibility 2

Ray's older. He can stay up late. Besides, it's a scary film. He can watch the film. You go to bed. I said go to bed. Do you hear? Sleep in Ray's room. Be quiet up there. No noise. Do you hear? Don't make a noise up there. You go to bed and be quiet. Ray can stay up. You don't want to watch Moby Dick, anyhow. It'll only scare you. I said go to bed. You've watched enough today. Sleep in Ray's room. Don't make a noise. It'll be on again. Wait till you're older.

Ken closes the door and goes upstairs. He's outside the bedroom door. Twenty steps away from the lounge. A stretch of fifteen stairs, then a small landing, then five more steps. It's the first door on the left; Ray's room.

Now there's talking. Television. Laughter. Serious voices. Comical voices. Television voices. The end of the programme. Adverts. Adverts. No, please. Don't start, not yet, not yet. Don't start. This is where they come out and say come down to watch the film. In a second. In a second that door down there will open and they'll all sing, Moby Dick's on. Come on now or you'll miss it. Hurry up. It's just starting.

So don't start yet, film. Wait. Don't start. Wait till they smile and say come on, come on in here and watch the film with us. Better hurry up there.

But there's the music. That's the music. They've stopped speaking. No laughing now. Now it's serious. Now they're watching the film begin. There's the sea. You can tell it's the sea. And there's the boat. You can hear the creak and groan of a boat. That's not scary. Please. Come on.

Close your eyes, and after three open them again. Three, two, one and that door opens. But there's the music. There's the sea music. There's the ship.

Come out of the room, someone, please. It's only just started. You can watch it now. We'll tell you what's happened. Ray will tell you. You do want to see the whale, don't you?

The whale.

But there's no voices now. Now there's no talking. Shhh. All listening. All watching. All quiet.

Sure. It's all right now. You're okay. You're in there. But look, here, outside the room, outside someone else's room. Don't touch anything. Just go to sleep. Go sleep on the blankets.

Look, I'm here.

Lie down and you can hear more. Lie down on the floor, and you'll be able to hear. It's dusty, this carpet. It's dark, holey, dusty, and it's loose. Look. You can pull it. You can see underneath. You can crawl underneath. Look. You can crawl along the landing under the carpet. There's just a few tacks, but they'll pull out. All the way along, right to the end. You can make it down to the next landing, down five stairs. Easy. Then back up again. Look. You can see through the holes in the carpet. You can see through where it's worn. There's two holes and you can see the front door. A carpet mask. Maybe you could stay quiet and they'll never find you. Gone under the carpet; under a dusty sea. If you stay really still then when they come they won't even see you. It's wood under here. Look. Feel the wood. Smell the wood. It creaks like a ship.

Moby. No.

Make it all the way to the bathroom and they'll come out and say, come on, Moby Dick's on. We've changed our mind. You can watch the film. It won't scare you. It's not too bad. Moby Dick's a good film. Come and sit here, between us. Or sit on the floor with Ray. Sit down there. Shift up a bit, Ray. Let him in there. They'll be patting cushions and smiling.

But this is the bathroom and they still haven't opened the door. There's no voices, just sounds of the sea and creaking boats. Maybe if you lift the carpet and make some noise. They've forgotten you. They've forgotten you're here. Ken. Up here on his own. Make some noise then they'll hear you and remember you want to watch the film. Stand up and waft the carpet. That's it. Just waft it. Look at that. It goes all the way down stairs in one huge tidal wave. All the way to the front door. Waft.

Waft another wave and a cloud of sea spray rises into the air. Waft. Look at all that spray. It's a whale, puffing out dust. Look at Moby Dick, here, in the hallway, up on the landing. It's Moby Dick everyone. Come and see Moby Dick under the sea. Waft, waft, waft.

Look. The air's thick with whale dust. You can hardly see the front door. Come on everyone. Come and see the whale out at sea.

55

It's me. It's me. It's me.

Then maybe the door opens and they say, come on in here, you, trouble. Come on in here with us and watch the film. That's right, you sit yourself down there. The whale's not even been on yet. I'll bet you thought we'd forgotten you, didn't you?

Ken blinks and his father's at the front door. He's taken off his belt, folded it in two and pulls it tight between his hands. Then he loosens it and cracks it together. Ken's holding the carpet and he's looking at his father. He closes his eyes and he's inside a stone on another planet. Inside the stone it's dark and dry and there's no whale dust anymore. Inside the stone it's nice and warm and quiet.

Lucy used to live round here, you know. She lived over the bridge, in Goole, but she was born out back, out that way. She was born in that small row of terraces near the peat works.

Try it. Take a right at the junction that's halfway between Goole and Swinefleet. Drive for a few miles, stop the car, get out and take a look. Get up on the side of the Gilberstone's Dike so you can get a couple of feet higher. Then you'll see Lucy. You'll see where she was born. Take a look out towards the peat works. Take a look south, towards the sun, towards that small line of trees. You'll feel the sun on your face. You'll feel its warmth. You'll squint a little or close your eyes, and the view will be gone. You're there, in the middle of nowhere, a couple of feet up above the fields, and that's about it. You're on your own, in the flattest of places and there's nothing separating you and the horizon besides thin air. There's nothing between you and Lucy.

Hydrological Cycle

Water covers over seventy percent of the earth's surface. Two hydrogen atoms and one oxygen atom. H_2O.

Scientists say the amount of water is constant. It doesn't increase, it doesn't decrease. That means if I drink it, pour it away, or boil it, the total amount, whether it's solid, liquid, or gas, remains constant. We can't get rid of water. It's not like oil. When we burn oil it disappears.

The amount of water, in total, doesn't alter. Sure, it rises up into the air. It evaporates from rivers and streams, forms clouds and rains down on us. But the total amount remains the same, so scientists say.

Water comprises over seventy percent of the human body. Over seventy percent of me has been around since the year dot. Seventy percent of me has been drunk by a woolly mammoth, has flowed down the Nile, has washed the face of Cleopatra. That's water. It's colourless, tasteless and odourless. It's forming those clouds you can see over there above that horizon.

Breathe in and you breathe in Lucy. She's vapour. She's in the air. She's floating around out the back of Old Goole. She evaporated off some concrete pavement and now she's forming a cloud or two in the distance. See those clouds over there? See that one that looks like it's dropped anchor out in that field? That's Lucy. She's way out over that way. Get up on Gilberstone's Dike and take a look.

I'd stopped at the traffic lights on the bridge. It was a hot day and I had the window wound down as far as it would go. The lights had just turned to red, so I knew I'd be there a while. It was one of those four way systems, the ones that seem to take forever to get back round to green.

I had my arm out of the window and as I drummed my fingers on the door I looked over to my right, at the silos. They were being filled with grain. I closed my eyes and thought about that sound. I wondered about the docks, the ships, about the silos and about the colour of the sky. I thought about Ken, and about what had happened. I couldn't help but think about it. It's all people have talked about for a while now. I breathed in deeply, held the air in my lungs then exhaled, slowly.

Relative Humidity

Ken loved dominoes. He was given a set one Christmas; an oblong wooden box with a sliding lid.

The dominoes were smooth and had a ceramic feel. Ken liked to clatter them together. He'd place them on the kitchen table, put his hands over them and swish them round and round.

Clatter, clatter. Clatter, clatter.

Then, one by one, he'd turn them over and join them together. Sixes next to sixes, fives next to fives, fours next to fours, threes next to threes, twos next to twos, ones next to ones and blanks next to blanks. He'd position them with great care, making sure the edges were always in line.

Then he'd turn them over again and swish them round.

Clatter, clatter, clatter, clatter.

When I opened my eyes again the traffic lights had changed. I looked over to the silos one more time before moving off. I wound up the window, a little, then drove over the blue bridge that leads to Old Goole. On the bridge I glanced down at the river. The water looked like it was flowing the wrong way, but then again it was only a glance.

I thought I might stop there, some day. I'll get out, spend some time on that bridge, take in the scene. I've thought the same each time I've driven out that way, but I haven't stopped, not once. There's plenty of things I've planned on doing.

Absolute Humidity

Ken's at the upstairs window. It's flat and empty out the back; just field after field after field. Out that upstairs window you can almost see to another planet.

The fact that it's so flat makes Ken seem even bigger. He sees himself in the field, out the back of the house. He's staring up at the sky. The wheat's up to his knees. The sky's a clear, icy blue.

Somewhere, somewhere out there, there's a silo being filled with wheat, or corn, or barley, or whatever. Somewhere out there Country and Western music is being played. Somewhere there's a woman out walking a cat on waste ground, there's a woman sitting at a Formica breakfast bar drinking tea. That's all happening. At any one moment all those things, all those events, all those sounds and movements occur.

But Ken? Ken's just fiction. He's only happening in the words of this page. Ken's not out in a golden field standing tall, staring at a cloudless sky. Ken's not in a field rattling dominoes together with a man who's twice his age. He's not staring into an empty fridge. No. Ken only exists in the words of this page.

Ken could quite easily disappear in the next sentence. He could walk into the river, he could fall into a big silver tube of dust and choke. He could evaporate, rise up into the clouds and rain down all over the world.

Or, he could close his eyes and fly off to another planet. He could disappear off the earth and inhabit a rock on the planet Keghyimlikazxeretwub. Ken could be in a rock on the planet Keghyimlikazxeretwub at this very minute. And from his rock he could be watching. He could be just watching from the safety of his rock. He could be watching and listening to what's going on.

To the right of the rock there's a sign stuck into the ground.

This is Planet
Keghyimlikazxeretwub

Ken can't pronounce Keghyimlikazxeretwub, so he calls it Kmb.

A factory ship can deal with a whale in no time at all. A whale's no problem. It can be caught, flensed, dismembered, butchered and pressure-cooked within the hour. A factory ship can have a whale meal ready in forty five minutes; from scratch. From swimming free in the ocean, to being harpooned and boiled; all within the hour. That's pretty good going when you're a thousand miles from anywhere.

If you have no appetite, then you can use the soap to wash your hands. Or you could wear some cosmetics, or perfume. It doesn't smell as you would imagine. No. There's no smell of the sea, of fish, or of a whale. There's no blood, no salt or slime. Sometimes, that whale ends up smelling of oranges or candy floss or something.

It's difficult to tell you what it was like. What I have is an interpretation; a story. It's a story that's been pieced together from all sorts of sources. You see, even if I was there with him, with Ken at the bar, I couldn't tell you exactly what it was like. No. He couldn't even tell you. He could do his best. Sure. He could give you some of the details and tell you something about what he felt and saw. He could tell you about the room and about the hundreds of people dancing in lines; forwards and backwards, backwards and forwards. He could tell you about the smell of leather and about the music. He could say about the smoke in the room, about silver heels tapping on the wooden floor and about plaster falling off the ceiling. Sure, he could tell you all that. He could tell you what Lucy looked like. He could give you some generalisation like she looked beautiful, and he'd really mean it, you know. He could say she had this look in her eyes that he can't describe. Sure, he could tell you a thousand things, but you could never feel what he felt. You could never see what he saw. You'd never go blind with his description of the sun; no matter how realistic it was. You'd need to look. Sure, you'd be able to understand what he meant. That's not in doubt. You could feel for him. You could sympathise with him.

This is just a map. It's a flat map littered with partial information. It's not letting you know all that much, really. Poor kid. The poor kid went out for the first time in his life. He may as well have gone to another planet.

Out in the fields, you see, he's all right. From way over there at the road or the river or the embankment you can't see how big he is. But in a crowded room, in the street, in the shops or wherever, he stands out real sharp. So he learned to stay away from people. He learned to be on his own.

That night though we'd arranged to meet up. It'd taken years to convince him *that he might get something from a night out at the club. It's not that he refused, point blank, each time. No. He just never agreed to come. He never said he wouldn't come, either. But that afternoon he finally nodded. He finally said, sure Alfie, sure I'll meet you.*

And there's me, just using him for pictures and words.

He could hear the music when he left the house. As he pulled the door shut he could hear the steel guitar in the air. They play the music loud in the club. You can hear it right across the river in Old Goole.

So that's how he got there. He closed the door and took a leap to the bar in the club. Lucy's in front of him. She's looking up at him and she's mouthing words at him.

Conditional Instability

They drank to it, Florrie and Lucy. They clinked their glasses together and laughed, real loud. Ken's at the bar, looking over at the wall or the window or something.

You won't do it, says Florrie.

Sure I will, says Lucy. How many times you seen me back down from something?

Florrie looks over at Ken. He's huge, she says. I never thought he was that big. I've never seen him so close up.

He's some giant all right.

So you'll do it?

Florrie. If I says I will, I will. Let me just have a touch more of this drink. I'll finish it off, then there's my excuse for going over.

Cheers, says Florrie. Cheers, says Lucy.

Bring me some evidence, says Florrie, and I'll be watching.

I know, says Lucy. And don't you worry. I will.

Lucy took hold of his hand and leaned back with all her weight. Ken hardly moved. He's standing with his left arm outstretched. She's holding onto him with both hands.

Come on big boy, she says. I know you want to dance. I'll bet you're a real good dancer, aren't you?

Ken looks at Lucy and breathes in deeply.

Lucy leans further back.

Come on. I know you want to. Come on.

Ken blinks. His lips are dry and he considers moistening them with his tongue. He studies Lucy's face and thinks some generalisations. Behind her people dance; line after line of them. The whole of Goole is in there, smiling and dancing and clapping together.

Lucy pulls harder. Her boots slip on the wood floor.

I'll get you up if it's the last thing I do, she says and she looks past Ken, over to the other side of the room.

Florrie waves. Lucy shimmies in close and wraps her arms round his waist. She sinks her face into his chest and undoes his belt.

It's difficult, talking to giants, she says. Then she looks right at him,

65

right into his eyes and says, you wonder whether they speak the same language.

She's unstable on her feet and stretches out a hand to the bar. Christ, why don't you speak? she says. Then she throws an empty glass down onto the chair behind him.

Ken just stood there like he wasn't even in the room. Florrie said he might as well have been a scarecrow or a windmill, or something and Lucy laughed and said, a scarecrow with pubes like a brillo pad.

Then she put her hand down his trousers. She laughed and came back from the bar with the drinks and told Florrie. She had one of his pubic hairs and she said, look.

So what's it like then? says Flo. Lucy tilts her head back, opens her mouth and laughs real loud. She shrieks and says she didn't get past the barbed wire. She says his hair was stiff and hard. She says, I thought I was going to lose my hand down there. Then she coughs and flicks the ash from her cigarette. She holds her hand up to her mouth for a moment and says, maybe there's a watchtower down there. Then she laughs out loud again.

Ken's over there, at the bar over near to the window. It's dark outside. He's motionless. The scene is still, like a painting or a photograph, but as you watch the picture changes. The colour fades and it all becomes a line drawing on a piece of paper. The scene simplifies itself. It eliminates the excess, all unnecessary information, all the surplus.

Ken's a continuous line, joined to the bar, joined to Lucy. One continuous line, touching him, touching her, touching the floor, touching the room.

One of Lucy's hands is down the front of his jeans, the other is in the air. It could be moving up to her mouth, it could be moving over towards him, it could be moving over to her cigarettes. Ken's looking straight at Lucy. His face is difficult to read. There's something in his look, whether it's in his mouth, or his forehead, or his eyes, it's difficult to tell. There's something about the way he is, the way he's stood.

Ken's a moment from looking away. You can see that's what he does. That's the way he is. He can only look for a while, a second, a moment, an atom of time, a fraction. And that single moment is held with him. There's no going back. There's no reversal, no escaping the new world.

Ken reaches out and lifts Lucy into his palm. She sinks into his skin. He feels her heart, he feels the blood race in her body but then she turns dead soft and dry like she's made of fluff or dust or flour.

The great whale has just gone below the surface of the black sea. He tilts his head down and sinks. That's what the whale does. His lungs are full of air. The whale can withstand enormous pressure. Down here there's no noise or traffic, there's no kettles or voices. Down here, here in the deep, it's silent.

He lays back, inhales then dives and disappears from view. Down into the dark; into the cold green sea.

When he's at the bottom he lays still. He's on the sea bed. Then, when the oxygen has been used, when his blood begins to boil, and his chest aches, he rises up from greeny-blackness towards yellowy light above him. He needs to release the air from inside. He rises up and plunges through the surface. The hot breath escapes and he draws in, heavily. The sun is on his back. He stays for a while, just watching, then dives again, down to the bottom of the sea.

Insolation

But then this isn't just about the three of them. No. It's as much about the river and the sky and the clouds and things, as it is about them. It's about this place, here. It's about the smallest things. It's about what it's like in the morning, in the dark, and about at night when the moon's out. It's about the way the river flows, and about why the river flows. It's about silver mud on the banks and about why this place is so flat. It's about blue and green. It's about rivers flowing up hill and it's about three people. It's about metal and tin and steel and copper and about the taste of rusty nails. It's about the smell of cigarettes and about damp wood. It's about the mud getting deeper and deeper. It's about being covered in silt, and sticky clay and sand and gravel. It's about the soil, and about tractors ploughing fields. It's about being still. It's feeling the weight of the atmosphere. It's about being a weather watcher. It's about listening for the tiny squeak of a tiny tin box. It's about staring across wide open spaces and about lying flat out on your back and looking at the stars. That's what it's about. It's about all of this. It's about three people. It's about Ken and Lucy, and Florrie. It's about the three of them. It's all round them. It's about not separating them from any place in the world. It's about being stuck in a river, or in a field, or on a bridge or any place you can think of. It's about being trapped inside of something. It's about being a giant. It's about not being able to breathe. It's about a quiet room in a small house and it's about no time at all. That's what it's about. It's about what happened. It's about standing still while everything shifts. It's about empty places and empty spaces. It's about this place, here. It's about the horizon being like a hoop around you. It's about mountains being ground to dust. That's what it's about. It's not just about Ken and Lucy and Florrie. No, it's not just about the three of them. It's about this place here; the flattest place on earth.

You wonder what it's like; having nothing on the inside. People said he's soulless. They said he's just a shell or a case or something. But that's not the way he is. He's no empty box. There's no empty boxes, not here.

I read this thing and it said if you cool a gas then at some point it turns to liquid. If it's cooled even further it turns solid. You know, if the atmosphere was cooled enough it'd become liquid. It's amazing. Makes you realise what we're living under. If it was cooled some more it'd become solid. Can you believe that? We're under this atmosphere of gases that could be a rock if it was cold enough.

Still, it doesn't feel like we're at the bottom of a gassy sea. Above us, up above the clouds and beyond, there's layers and layers and layers of gases. It's miles high. It's difficult to say where it stops because it gets so diffused, so rarefied. But way up there, at some point, the atmosphere comes to an end. Maybe six or seven hundred miles up there is the very top. And we're right at the bottom of it all. We're right under that mass of gas and dust and water and ice and clouds and salt and light and energy and wind and things. There's tonnes of stuff above us.

When you're a kid they tell you there's more stars in the universe than grains of sand on all the beaches in the world. Just think, those countless billions of stars might be pressing down on us too. We can't see the half of it, never mind feel it. On a still day in summer we wouldn't even know it's all there. We don't lie out in fields and feel the weight of the universe pressing down on us.

Sure, we see the rain and the clouds. We see blue skies and the sun. We feel the force of the winds. And we know the universe is there all right because it keeps us awake at night by rattling the glass in the windows. But we don't wake up and feel there's been a slight change in pressure. No. We just pull back the curtains and wonder what the day's like. If we've got a barometer on the wall we go up to it, set the needle, tap the glass. We hum to ourselves, or tut, or sigh as the needle shifts one way or the other. The weather's going to change, we say. Sure it is. The weather's always changing.

You know, we see a blue sky because sunlight is scattered by dust and gas and things when it travels through the atmosphere. It gets scattered, and when it splits the blue part of the spectrum falls down towards us. That's the way it works, so they say. Apparently, that's why we see different colours later on, when the sun's setting. It's because the light's scattered at a slightly different angle. But it's not blue, not real blue. There's no blue curtain hanging up there. It's not something you can touch, or feel, or smell. You see the sky and the sky is blue. That light's travelled ninety million miles from the sun in just a few minutes. And on its way through the atmosphere it's clattered around and when it's clattered around some blue light gets scattered down to the fields out the back of Old Goole. A bit lucky, I suppose, if you're out in those fields looking up at a copper coloured sun.

Seems like there's blue behind everything.

The pressure on us, the pressure on barometers and on tin boxes all round the world, is atmospheric pressure. But sure, you know that.

A forecaster might use a number of things to tell if the weather's going to change. One way of doing so is by using an aneroid barometer. An aneroid barometer's one of those things that's made of dark, heavy wood. It's got a big round face with a glass cover. You tap the glass to see if the needle shifts. The needle shifts one way for high pressure, the other for low pressure.

Inside the instrument there's this tiny box, a partially evacuated box, and that's the thing that responds to subtle changes in pressure. It's a box that's had almost all the air removed. That means the box is more responsive. If pressure increases the weight of air on the box increases and the box collapses. If pressure decreases, the box expands. Simple.

The box is attached to an arm that's attached to the needle that gives the reading on the face of the barometer. On top of one needle is another. If you want to know what the weather's doing, you set one needle over the other, then tap the glass. Then the partially evacuated box either expands or collapses. The arm moves. The needle moves. With the shift you can see from the marker needle what's happening.

The needle shifts and we think it's going to rain, or there may be snow, or hail, or it may get windy, or, if we're lucky, we might get some sunshine. But inside, under the glass, beneath that round white face that's been staring out at us for years and years, there's something that's responding to even the most subtle of changes. It shows us what's going to happen. Sure, we could do nothing. We could just tap the glass and sigh. We can stare at our reflection in the glass. We can stand in front of the barometer and watch the needle move one way, then the other. You know, clouds jump, the weather changes, pressure changes.

Outside, the weather's changing.

Inside, the box is collapsing.

You might think that crushing the box would bring bad weather; like wind, clouds and rain. But it doesn't. No. Crush the box and the weather's good. Crush the box and you get blue skies. Crush the box and, summer or winter, the sun's out, the sky has fluffy white cotton ball clouds and there's no wind. Everything's still. Clouds don't move, the trees don't budge. Crush the box and you take the breath out of the air. Crush the box and things seem to get better. The weather does, that is. Ridiculous, I suppose.

Expand the box though and that's when you get wet and windy weather. Expand the box and that's when the winds increase in speed. Expand the box and the air in the atmosphere becomes unstable, it rises, it forms clouds. That's when you get rain; heavy rain. That's when the sky turns grey. That's when the sky shifts quickly across the fields. That's when the weather really gets to you. That's when the grey above you churns and swirls. That's when things become really unpredictable.

Take a tin out of a cupboard and watch it. That small tin of soup or condensed milk, or whatever it is you have, is expanding and contracting every day.

Throw a tin can from a rooftop and watch it split open on the pavement. Watch the insides pour over the concrete and into the gutter. Stand up there, raise your arms up into the air and watch as the thick white liquid runs down the grid. Watch it drip away. Watch until the can's empty. If you could reach down and lift the can it'd be real light now. You wonder what to do, whether to leave it where it fell, or take it away. But, in the end, you just don't really do that much at all. You're on a rooftop with your arms up above your head and all around you the weather is changing.

Jet Streams

It's dark when I set off for work. The ground's slippery. It's like the middle of the night or something. It's cold. There's no one around. Streets are empty. That's what it's like round here. There's a concrete pavement on this side of the road, but on the other, over there, is the river. You can't see it from here, even in the day. It's deep down in the channel, maybe six feet or so below you. It'd have to flood for you to see it.

There's no wall or barrier at the sides of the river. No. You just cross the road and walk over to the grass verge. Just beyond the grass the land dips down. That's where the river is. It's there now; slow and lifeless.

Just to the left of here's the bridge that joins Old Goole to Goole. It's wide enough for traffic to flow one way or the other, but not for it to flow both ways at the same time. Now though, it's quiet. The lights go from red to amber to green but there's no cars. It's too early for cars.

Over that way's the docks. In the day they're busy. Cranes swing round. Ships get unloaded. Trucks come and go. Containers get lifted and shifted. Silos get filled, silos get emptied. Things arrive and things get taken away. From here it's simple. From here there's no problems, no mistakes. From here, by the bridge, everything's smooth and seamless. From here everything falls into place.

It's wider than it seems, this dike. When you drive over it, it seems pretty insignificant. But when you stand on the bridge, when there's a spring tide and it's been raining hard, when the water's flowing the wrong way, when it's coming from the east, flowing uphill to the west rather than from over there where the ground's buckled and twisted, the river seems all that much wider.

When it's like that the water comes just a few feet from the road. Then, it's wide and fast and smooth. If it didn't flow as fast you'd think you could swim it.

You know, it smells different depending on which way it flows, this river. It's oily when it flows east, salty when it flows west. You can hear it, too, when it's high in the banks. You hear it swish by like a curtain.

Now though, the river's low. It's been dry for the last week, and there's a neap tide. When the river's low in the banks the flow's irregular. But

73

don't get me wrong, the river's still unnatural looking. Sure, the banks are straight, but when it's low you see how the water goes in spirals. It zigzags from side to side. The zigs and the zags are far apart, maybe fifty feet or so, but the pattern's there; the spirals are there. The water flows to the left, then to the right, like it's rocking. Seems things don't go much for straight lines. Even in an unnatural place like this, that much is true.

At the moment it's just about light enough to see the water. There's a few speckles of silver on the surface. Sometimes though you can see much more. Stand on the south side of the river, when the sun's low in the sky and you can see the tallest things: cranes, warehouses, ships. Sometimes, when there's a breeze, those reflections sway around. On that surface they're all moving in line, all in time. It's like they're dancing some slow dance.

Further down that way, just beyond where it curves to the right, the banks have been built up. The river over that way is the Ouse. That's a good name for a river. The Ouse. The Ouse bends. It meanders. The road bends. The river bends.

You drive along a meander as you drive from Old Goole to Swinefleet. You drive along next to the smallest rise that's the biggest rise round here. Stand in the fields, look towards the river and you just see this rib along the distance. It's like the land's been starved. It's like it's been thinned out to leave the bones showing through. But that's the Ouse. That's the so called natural part of the river. This is the dike. This is the Dutch River. This is the straight part. This part was dug out a hundred and eighty years ago to form this gully. That's where Goole gets its name from.

Sure, you can see a lot from here. You just need to stop sometime and take a look.

Florrie's been stuck in the mud for as long as I remember. This water flows by every day. Now and then the tide comes in and the water flows the other way. The river rises. Florrie's submerged. You think sometimes she'll be gone when the river subsides. But when it does she's still there. She looks different now than she did a year or two ago, but from yesterday there's hardly a change. The river swells, she gets wet, the sun comes out, she dries out some. She never gets completely dry though.

74

Not even on the hottest day of the year, when the river's like a snail trail at the bottom of the banks or when the mud's dry and cracked does she get completely dry.

Sometimes, you know, I've been over to the other side of the river and I've walked down the bank to the edge of the mud. She's bigger than she looks from the bridge, but she's still thin. She's well worn by the water. I've been right up close to her, but I couldn't touch her because the mud was too deep. I tried to get closer still, but that greasy, oily mud was getting over my boots. She was over there, just out of reach.

I shouted to her, but she didn't budge. Maybe I see how she was when she was young. Maybe she's not like that any more. Maybe the mud's meant to cover her. Maybe she chose to be in the mud. Maybe she wants it to get deeper and deeper. I'm sure I don't know.

All I do know is this mud's over my boots. There's lines of purple and yellow all over them. So I head back to the bank and when I get back to the bank I sit on the grass. She's facing away from me now. I could throw a stone over that way to attract her attention but she wouldn't look round, not for something as insulting as that. So I sit a while and watch her.

Florrie, I say. Florrie. Over here. Look.

The water down there's dark. I can see the bed. It's smooth. I wonder what she's thinking about. I wonder what she's looking at. Maybe her eyes are closed. Maybe she'll turn round and look up at the bridge, or over that way to Old Goole, but she's never done it before, not that I've seen. Not once.

She doesn't look round so I go back to the bridge. My boots are caked so I knock them against the bricks. I kick one foot then the other against the wall. My hands are on the metal rail. I'm looking down at my boots. I'm watching small pieces of wet silt and clay fall from them. I'm here, on the bridge. There's no one else around. There's no traffic, no wind, no noise from the docks. The clouds are still in the sky. To my right there's a row of houses. One or two have lights on, the rest are dark. To the left there's the docks. It's dark over that way. It's late. Everything's a mix of purple and mustard and grey and black. I wonder what I must look like, some old man, all alone, kicking the wall on such a chilly night.

I was thinking last night about the river. I'd read about gangrene. I'd read about how the blood is slowly cut off to the infected area, and that the skin turns black. It made me think of the Dutch River. But then maybe I'm being harsh. It's been dark for months now, and when I cross the bridge it's early morning or evening. Either way, it's dark. There's no light to reflect on the surface. Sometimes there's the moon. But more often than not it's cloudy. There's no stars, no natural light. I look down at the river and the river's black. It's so black you don't know if it's moving.

Doldrums

Florrie has a splinter in her rib. She gets a pain in her side when she walks, when she drinks, when she laughs. If she's sitting on the chair in the kitchen she'll rub her side, her left side, and she'll say her rib's giving her gyp. She fell over one time. She came into the kitchen just after Lucy had knocked over a bowl of soup and she slipped and landed on her side. She blames the pain in her side on that fall. That fall was a year ago. She rubs her side and says the bone's moved again. She draws in breath heavily but it's like she can't fill her lungs, like her chest can't expand enough to take in the air. She gasps, but the air's leaking out from between her ribs. She rubs just below and to the side of her left breast. She runs a finger in between two ribs. She feels for the splinter, for the scratch, for the lump, the bruise, or whatever it is. Sometimes she finds the pain and keeps her finger on it. She presses and the pain increases.

She's on the bridge that crosses the dike. Florrie leans over the side and looks directly down at the water. She touches the ribs on the left side of her chest and breathes in deep. She can't quite fill her lungs. She coughs. Her eyes water. She feels the small splinter in her side.

She looks at the water and she spits.

I knew someone who slept round at her place one time. He wasn't with her, he was with Lucy. This guy said that they'd got into bed, him and Lucy. He said he was on top of her. Lucy was just wearing her knickers and she had this real sad expression or worried look or something on her face. Then she said she didn't want to do anything and she asked if he minded. This guy said, no. No, he didn't mind at all. They could hear Florrie in the next room. She was with this young guy and the bed head was beating real hard against the wall. Lucy turned onto her side and switched off the bedside lamp.

This friend of mine said he laid down, nestled into her back and fell asleep.

Florrie's on the bridge and she's thinking. She's looking east. Behind her the sun's setting. Behind her there's a low band of orange and red light in the sky. But Florrie doesn't look.

Florrie's a piece of wood stuck in the mud. You can see her from the bridge. She's thin. She was thrown from the bridge and she landed there at the side of the river. She thought she'd get out, someday. She thought she'd just be able to step to the side, walk up to the embankment and go up to the bridge. But no. She's still there. She's sinking, and the mud's getting deeper.

It's been raining for two days now. The horizon gets closer when it rains like this. I can just about see the trees at the bottom of the field. There's no depth any more. Lucy lost her perspective when she got wrapped in cellophane. Florrie's in the mud. Ken's at the window. The sky's one dimensional. Everything's too big round here. Everything's too flat. Everything's too empty.

I had a friend who was writing a book. He'd given the main characters some shape, but he wanted more, he wanted something else. He was sitting, willing the people to move, but they wouldn't. It was like they'd become frozen. Ken at the bedroom window. Lucy at the kitchen table. Florrie on the bridge. The three of them motionless.

Last night, this friend of mine sat on a rocky cliff and watched the sunset. The air was still. The sea was black, waveless. He'd sat and watched as the sun showed off in the distance. It was like some rare bird, puffing itself up, slowly revealing all its colours. He was alone and he thought about Ken and Lucy. He pictured them in his mind's eye, and he willed them to move, to speak, to act in some way. But they refused. They were solid.

The writer felt as though he needed to know more about them. If he knew more, if he knew how they thought, how they behaved, then perhaps they would spring into life. Perhaps the ice would melt and they would move again.

The next day he sat at his typewriter and wondered about what to write. Ken's at the bedroom window. Lucy's at the kitchen table. Just blink, he thought. Just blink and something might happen. But they refused. They refused the words he tried to put into their mouths, they refused the thoughts he tried to put into their heads.

So he picked them up and shifted them. Two cardboard cut-out people. Two people turned solid and lifeless. Unmoving, unblinking.

The writer placed them one on top of the other. Both were stiff, lacking in depth. He moved Ken from the window and put him in another place. Put him in another place, he thought, and see what happens. But nothing did happen. Ken remained stiff and solid. In the chair at the front of the house, in the fields round the back, over the road by the dike, on the roof of his house; nothing happened. Ken wouldn't move.

Lucy was the same. The writer took her from the kitchen; but she remained frozen. He tried to push them together but they were still. Nothing changed. Nothing happened. No movement occurred.

He listened for a while, and thought about the sound of their voices. He thought about how Ken would sound. Say a word, he thought, just say a word and from that word something may spring out and the story may continue. Blink an eye, smile, breathe. But no matter how hard he tried he couldn't get him to speak. There was no breath in his lungs, no words in his mouth, no thoughts in his head.

Only last week they'd lain together in a field; Ken and Lucy. But that was a week ago when his mind ran smoothly like a river. The characters were alive then.

Their hair and fingernails grew, mouths smiled, skin aged, eyes watered, tears fell. He could see it all in them. He heard their voices in a boiling kettle, in the tap of a drum, in the clatter of a drawer. Only last week Lucy sat with Florrie and they'd smoked and talked, and smoked and talked. They'd shopped in town, got wet in the rain, drank tea in Rose's Cafe. That was last week, when clouds drifted past the kitchen window, when the wind blew hard against the glass. That was when blues turned to whites, turned to yellows, turned to greys. Last week, everything was mobile, everything was all free. Lucy was in the kitchen. She sat at the Formica breakfast bar and smelled the chicken soup she'd made for lunch. Clouds of chicken flavoured steam rose from the pan. The lid opened and closed like a small steel mouth. She watched the lid, watched the steam rise up into the air and she smiled. She had an ache in her stomach like she'd not felt since before people walked on the moon.

But that was last week. This is this week. This is today. This is now. And now, things are different.

The writer looked out of the window and saw a black tractor moving in the distance. He saw a series of horizontal lines. A line of hazel trees marked the far distance. Then there were telephone wires strung between poles. Then field boundaries, one after the other, line after line of yellow and gold. Then the ditch that ran along the near field, then the road. Then, finally, the base of the window. Line after line, all smooth, all even, all dead straight. One, two, three, four and more. Left to right, right to left, one behind the other to the horizon. Beyond that the sky offered no extra dimension, no alternative. It was white and grey and pasty, like some poorly developed photograph.

The writer looked up and watched the tractor in the far distance move from right to left. He looked back down at the blank page and Ken moved.

Relative Humidity

Ken's in the chair that's directly in front of the mantelpiece and he's looking to his left, over to the window. The grey of the day has gone. Now, high up, there's some thin, wispy cirrus clouds. The sky's a sharp piercing blue. This window faces north. From the chair you can't see over to the docks. No. From the chair you can see the road, the grass verge and the corrugated iron warehouse that stores the grain that's been shipped in from Poland. He looks away and focuses on the mantelpiece. His arms rest on the sides of the chair. There's a rumble as a heavy truck goes past. Ken stands up and goes over to the window.

The truck's at the traffic lights, over that way to the left. The engine churns out dark smoky fumes. Ken places the tips of his fingers against the glass.

Now, he can see over to the docks. It's late Spring. Twenty blue cranes, all almost as tall as the spire on the church, lean at the same angle.

To the left is the grain works. Tall silos, squat silos, tubeways and walkways. A still, quiet place. Spots of artificial light. The river's flowing from right to left; uphill. It's high in the banks.

The traffic lights change, the truck moves off and turns right over the bridge. It continues towards the docks, past the silos, then it disappears behind the wall by the Vermuyden Hotel.

Ken stands a while longer. Looks like the weather's going to change, he thinks. He breathes in deeply. Yes. It's definitely going to change.

Snow

Lucy's hair is dry. She styles it, then sprays it solid. It has the feel of candy floss and sticks to your hand if you pat it. Ken likes the smell of Lucy's hair. It reminds him of something from when he was young

When Lucy was young her hair was light and wavy. She has a photograph on the sideboard from when she was twenty one. She's sitting on the bonnet of an Austin 1100. She's wearing flat canvas pumps and light coloured trousers. The trousers are short, tight. On top she's wearing a pale blue T-shirt. Her hair is long and she's leaning back. One leg is cocked up, foot on the bonnet, the other dangles down. It's the day that Neil Armstrong set foot on the moon. The twentieth of July, 1969.

It said on the weather news that some dust and sand had been picked up from the Sahara desert by the wind and had been blown high up across Europe. It's been causing more rain than normal. It's given the rain a reddish tinge and has left stains down the windows.

It rained early this morning. First in heavy bursts, then less intense. Then it fell as light drizzle. Now, the sun's out from behind those blue-grey clouds and the wind has died down.

This next part starts in Ken's house. I know it's confused. I know it jumps around from place to place. It goes from the kitchen to the hallway to the bedroom then out into the fields. It takes turns here and there. It's not all neat and ordered like Ken wants it to be. No. He's tried to straighten it out but the pieces don't fit that well together. Instead, it's all crooked. Poor kid.

You know what it is about this? It's that it makes Ken seem different than he really is. It makes it seem like he's spent a lifetime with Lucy when it hasn't really been any time at all. Sure, I know that. But this is how it is when he remembers what happened. He's played it over and over, piece by piece. It's not one continuous sequence of events. His memory's not cut into the landscape, it's not straight, like the Dutch River. No. His memory's like the Ouse. It meanders. It twists and curves. It flows one way, then the other, then curls in on itself. It clouds over and silts up. It uncovers things he thought were long since dead and buried.

Ken thinks about Lucy when he sees a pair of boots, when he sees a grey sky, when the wind blows against the windows. His mind jumps and he's in the kitchen, in the fields, or upstairs in the bedroom. For sure, he thinks about what's happened. He remembers, and every time he does his memory changes. But you know this wasn't exactly like it happened. You know Ken's not like this. Maybe he's changed it around some over time. All he knows is his memories are getting thinner. It's like they're evaporating, and are off forming clouds somewhere. That's the way it is. Memories aren't set in concrete. Memories don't weigh anything at all. They're lighter than air. They're as light as those clouds over there. But you know about that, don't you?

Electric Storms

Tea's fine, she says. Tea's fine.

They go through to the kitchen. Lucy sits at the table. It's a small chipboard table with a yellow surface. The legs of the table are thin, loose. As she sits the table wobbles. She places her bag on the floor next to her chair and lights a cigarette. She looks at Ken, crosses her legs then smiles.

Ken takes the kettle to the sink. He turns the tap. The tap glugs as the water arrives. He fills the silver pot through the spout. A few drops spray onto the side and onto his shirt as he holds it under the running water. He places it on the stove, turns the gas and presses the ignition switch. It clicks four or five times, then the gas lights. Lucy watches him, then looks down at the table top. There's some crumbs from biscuits or crackers over the other side from where she's sitting. She sweeps them together into a neat pile. Next to the crumbs is the skin from a lemon and a few grains of sugar. She moves her tongue across the roof of her mouth then touches her lips.

The gas burns. The water begins to hiss and rumble. She gazes back to Ken.

Ken's over near the sink. He's staring out of the window. Lucy watches him, then looks round the room again.

The floor has a lino surface. The lino's dog eared at the points where it meets the units. In front of the fridge the lino is dark, like it's almost worn through. It's a small dark space, slightly wider than Ken's feet, almost perfectly circular. There's a unit to her left, on top of which sits the fridge. Another, to the right, next to the cooker, is older looking. In between the two, below the window, is the sink. The sink is yellowy-white, enamel, deep set, heavy. At either side of the sink there's a small work surface. One side has a mug, a silver plate, and cutlery. The other has a cardboard box. From where Lucy's sitting, she can't see inside. Above her head is a wood cabinet painted dark green. There's no lamp-shade on the bulb that hangs from the wire in the centre of the ceiling.

Ken lifts the mug, turns it over and places it on the side next to the kettle. He returns to the sink and moves the knives, forks and spoons around until he finds a teaspoon. He takes it to where he'd placed the mug and drops it inside. He gazes down at his feet, looks back up to the mug, then removes the spoon and positions it on the surface in a perfect straight line pointing away from him. He sees his reflection in the spoon. He sees his chest, shoulders and head. The image is inverted, it's thin and elongated. He turns the spoon over and his reflection is the right way up. His face is wider, shorter. His neck shrinks, his chest widens. The image is silvery grey. He sinks into the spoon. He sinks into the bowl, into the silver basin. Then he turns the spoon and he rolls over silver mountains. He's a stream flowing down a mountain side, rushing down into valleys, down into the green sea.

Sometimes he can speak, you know. Sometimes words fall like notes from a violin. But then sometimes he's a whale screaming under water. Sometimes his throat dries and sharpens so he sounds like a rusty saw being scraped with a nail. His voice disappears and he can only scratch at something inside. He wants it to be smooth. He wants to be able to say what he means. But that doesn't happen. Not with Ken.

The kettle boils. Steam rises from the spout and Ken lifts it from the stove. He doesn't feel the heat from the handle. He fills the mug and the cup, replaces the kettle and turns off the gas.

Ken walks over to the fridge. He places his hand on the handle and the world stops revolving as he stares at the fridge door. Lucy freezes in her chair. The steam solidifies. The colour fades from the scene and they become two simple drawings in a book. Two line drawings on a piece of paper.

You seem to like clouds, says Lucy.

Ken raises a hand to his mouth and coughs. Lucy looks at him, then she points up into the air.

I was told once that an average sized cloud has enough water to fill a thousand swimming pools. Can you believe it? She says. A thousand swimming pools.

Ken gazes out of the window.

Have you felt the weight of a bucket of water? She says. A bucket of water makes your arm ache. Lucy leans forwards. She looks at Ken, then stares up, out of the window.

Imagine holding up millions of the things. All that weight up there,

85

she says. One's enough for anyone, isn't it?

Lucy waits a while then says, you know, I was told that sometimes clouds just drop right out of the sky.

Ken leans further forwards, against the sink. Over in the distance, beyond the fields, beyond the small line of trees, there's a band of bright silver clouds in a light blue sky.

Tonnes of water, says Lucy. All in one big lump. Like one big fat raindrop. She glances at Ken, then smiles a thin smile. You'd better watch that sky when you're out walking in those fields. You'd better watch one of those clouds doesn't fall right out of the air and land on top of you. She laughs quietly and the chair rocks from side to side.

Global Circulation

I want to give you something, she says. Here.

Lucy undoes a bead necklace. How about you take this, she says.

She reaches up, puts her arms round his neck and fastens the catch. She's up close to him, looking into his eyes.

Green and silver and grey and blue. I saw those colours on the back of a truck that was going to the docks. There was this thing on the truck, like a tube or something. It was early morning and the sun was behind me.

I was up close to the truck and the colour on the tube changed with every twist and turn in the road. I wondered if it was because the road wasn't straight and the tube caught the light in different ways. It took on a kind of tobacco orange colour at one point, then changed to greeny, silver-blue. It was like the sky. Up there, behind me, was a star or two, and the sun was rising. The sky was fine, delicate looking, silver and blue, and just above the horizon was a long thin patch of orange. I followed the truck round a couple more bends and over the bridge. Then it turned off to the left, towards the docks. I continued to the lights and took a right. As I drove the sun rose and the sharpness of the morning evaporated as the day became warmer.

Mirage

They're in the hallway and they're dancing. Ken's arm's around Lucy's waist and they're moving in circles. He follows her lead. One foot forwards, then back. Shift body weight onto the other foot, then spin round. Left foot forwards, then back, then back to the right again.

Lucy holds Ken's left hand. She smiles, laughs and exaggerates her movements. She moves up close, presses her body against his, then moves back, lets go of his hand and takes hold of his waist. She glides from side to side like she's lighter than air.

Ken steps forwards and shifts his weight. Lucy swivels round and round and raises her arms like a Flamenco dancer. She pouts and blows him a kiss. Ken's melting as his shoulders rock from side to side. His head bobs up and down. Lucy moves in close again and puts her hands on his hips.

See, she says. Knew you'd like it.

Lucy steps back, twirls, then looks up at him. Are we going to keep going round and round in circles?

Ken pulls her in close and says, I don't know what else to do.

This track's Nat King Cole's, Let's Face the Music and Dance. They've got the music up loud and they're really dancing. Lucy's got a glass in her left hand, she's smiling.

Watch you don't spill it, she says. Then she pulls him into a tango and they tango down the hallway to the front door. They spin round and tango back to the kitchen. Lucy stops and takes a drink of gin. Ken sits down.

There's no ice left, she says. Damn it. They should run a delivery service from Hodgson's. Give them a ring. Tell them we want buckets of the stuff.

The song finishes and there's a silence before the next track.

Now someone's singing Cry Me a River.

Lucy burps then says, this is sad this one. I like the ones that make you want to dance. She curls her bottom lip and looks at him. This sounds like we should have the lights down low, like we should be in some smoky room somewhere.

Then she says she thought they were all supposed to be famous songs and Ken says he can't believe she's never heard this one before. Where've you been? he says and he shakes his head.

Lucy takes another drink of gin and wags a finger. Now if only I could sing like this, she says.

Then she sighs and says, it's too sad, this one, and she goes and presses the button that sends the music back a track. Come on. Let's dance again.

She places her glass on the table and unzips her boots. Ken watches closely as she removes them. She's wearing light brown tights and she's got a hole where a toe pokes through. Lucy looks at Ken, pulls her skirt up above her knees, wraps her arms round her waist, and dances with herself.

Now she's got her eyes closed. It's like she's not in the kitchen anymore. She dances through the whole song and then when the music stops she opens her eyes.

You've been watching me, she says and she steps forwards and brushes her lips against his cheek.

Ken smiles and says she'd better wind it on before the sad one starts again.

Now where'd I put the box? she says.

Then the music stops. Ken hears Lucy humming softly. He looks up, out of the window. It's a light, bright morning. There's a small white cloud in a clear blue sky. Ken watches it for a while, then looks round, into the hallway, towards Lucy. The beam of light from the skylight lights up the space between them. Ken focuses on dust; rising and falling, rising and falling.

The music starts up again. It's someone singing Fly Me To The Moon. Ken watches as Lucy closes her eyes and sings along. She has a beautiful voice. He can hear her over the music. She's at the end of the hallway, near the door and she's moving slowly from side to side. She hugs herself, opens her eyes and looks at him. She knows all the words, all the way through.

Ken's stood now, just outside the kitchen doorway.

In other words, sings Lucy as the song ends. In other words. I, love, you.

Ken waits a moment, then says, Bravo. Bravo, Lucy. Bravo.

Another track starts. Lucy walks over to him.

You sit down, she says. She smiles and curls some of his hair between her fingers. She leans over the table and takes hold of her glass.

Ken smells the perfume on her neck. The perfume's sweet, like oranges. Lucy sees him inhale and kisses him on the top of his ear.

Wow, you've got hairy ears, she says. I think you've got the hairiest ears in the world.

He puts a finger into his ear and brushes it around. Get me the case, says Ken. This is show time.

That's not like Ken. You don't imagine him saying the things he says. You don't imagine him doing the things he does. He's Ken. He's big. He doesn't dance and make a fool of himself. He doesn't fall in love. That's not the way he was built. That's not the sort of thing that happens to him. Not Ken. Not Ken there, dancing. No.

Weatherman

Ken looks over the songs and says for her to put on the sixth track.

What is it?

Just you wait and see, says Ken.

Lucy burps, places her drink on the floor and fingers with the control. Ken takes a mouthful of gin from the bottle then stands up.

Ready? she says.

Ken claps his hands together. Ready.

Lucy presses the play button and a double bass starts. Then comes some clapping and a piano. Then there's something that's like a tapping or clicking noise.

Ken's in front of her and he starts this kind of shuffle thing with his feet like he's Fred Astaire or someone. He's leaning one way, then the other, then he turns round and goes from side to side. Lucy's cross-legged on the floor in the hall and she's clapping in time with the music. She brushes a strand of hair from her eyes and says, Go, Ken. Go.

She turns the music up louder and Ken starts to bob up and down. He leans over to the left then to the right. He's shuffling and turning round and round. He's really got it in time with the music. He's right there, right on the beat and Lucy's clapping and she's shouting, Yeah. Go, Ken. Go.

Ken kicks his big legs up into the air like they're weightless. It's Dave Brubeck, he shouts and Lucy claps and smiles and Ken's dancing and dancing and dancing into the beam of light.

Some people like bird watching or stamp collecting. Some people like train spotting or fishing. You know Ken. You know what he likes. He just wants to watch the horizon. Sure, he's a horizon watcher, a weather watcher, a cloud watcher. I'm not dead sure what it is he's looking at. But there's something over there that keeps him hooked for hour after hour after hour. I've stood next to him sometimes and looked where he's looking. I've looked and seen the sky and the clouds and the fields. Sure, I look out there, too. But he looks, really looks, and he doesn't say a word.

You see what happened? This machine would pick up something, some images or sounds from out that way, but then it'd just flick to another place, another time. It could have been an hour later. It could have been the next day or twenty years ago. It was like all this stuff, all these memories were in the air, like they were in the clouds. It was like those clouds were made of millions of fragments of memories. I don't know. I really don't know how it happened.

Shooting Stars

Lucy raises her clenched fist to her mouth and coughs. I'm worn out, she says. I can hardly breathe. I feel like my legs are dropping off.

She's holding a pair of Ken's boots. Here, he says. Take these.

He handed her the boots with tread that's worn flat, with leather that's all scuffed.

I can't wear these, she says.

Put them on, says Ken.

Lucy leans forward and massages her foot. She curls her toes as she rubs them. Ken can smell her feet. He breathes in deeply, quietly. His lungs fill with air and he holds his breath for a moment before exhaling.

Don't watch me, she says. You'll make me nervous.

This is ridiculous, she says. She slips on the right boot, leans back and pulls the lace tight. I can't walk all the way out there in these.

You can do it, he says. Put them on. Tie the laces and pull them in tight. I'll carry you if you get tired.

I even got to see myself, you know. I focused in on a cloud and slap bang in the middle of it all was me, there at the kitchen table.

Warm Air

It's chicken soup, she says. How many times do I need to tell you?

She drops the spoon into the bowl then pushes the bowl forwards an inch or so across the table. She's still wearing her coat, hat and scarf. The coat's buttoned up to the neck and I wonder whether I've seen her at the table like this before.

I take a sip of soup and say, I know it's chicken soup. I know it is. Then she closes her eyes and speaks as though I'm foreign or deaf or something.

Last night, she says, we had roast chicken. We had potatoes, peas, carrots and gravy. For your sandwiches, today, you had chicken. You know full well I make soup from what's left over. We do it every week, and every week you say the same thing. I wouldn't mind but you ask as though you've never tasted chicken soup before in your life.

She sits still for a moment. Then she speaks, but she doesn't look at me. You have tasted it, she says. I know you have. You've had this soup over and over.

Now she's got her eyes closed again and her head's tilted, away from me. It's hopeless, she says.

Rapid Terrestrial Radiation

So, says Lucy. We've had books and films and colours. She's on the ground, next to Ken. She's in the grass and her eyes are closed.

What about an animal? If it was an animal what would it be?

Ken thinks for a while. He feels Lucy move slightly. He's standing straight. He's standing exactly at her middle, to her right, a fraction from her hip.

It's a whale, he says.

Tell me, she says as she squeezes his ankle.

What about a game then? she says. If it was a game what would it be? She rubs up and down on the back of his boot. She pulls on the lace that's wrapped tight round the top of his ankle.

That's easy, he says. Snakes and ladders.

Lucy's got some straw between her lips. She feels the end with her tongue. The end's stiff and dry. She presses with her teeth. She feels the surface give a little, then she rolls the straw from one side of her mouth to the other. She takes the straw from her mouth, looks at Ken and squeezes his ankle.

You look like you're ready for lift off, says Lucy.

As I said, Lucy's laid out flat, Ken's to her right. Lucy stares up at the sky. Ken stares straight ahead. He's stood still. From her position Ken looks bigger than ever.

What you looking at? she says. Lucy shades her eyes from the bright blue sky and the midday sun.

Ken breathes in deeply, holds the air in his lungs, then exhales slowly.

I was just thinking, he says.

So tell me, says Lucy.

She's got the straw between her lips again. Now and then she removes it and rolls it softly between her fingers.

You're going to take root if you stand there any longer, she says. Sit yourself down. Lucy pats the ground to her left, squeezes the straw and closes her eyes.

The sun's burning hot today.

I was going to tell you that Ken kisses Lucy's ankle. But it's not as simple as that. Lucy's lying down and Ken's down, by her side. He's holding her leg. She's got the sun on her face and her eyes are closed. Ken's kneeling on the soil next to Lucy. He raises her leg up to his mouth and brushes his lips along her skin, along the bone that leads down to her ankle. He kisses her ankle, then her right knee. Then he moves higher and kisses her shoulder. He kisses her elbow, then her knuckles, then the tips of her fingers.

Convection 1

Layer after layer, one on top of the other. The most recent is sea green, turquoise. Underneath is the colour of sour milk. Beneath that there's reddy pink, then black. Still deeper and there's pock-marked metal that's been hammered with nails. Thousands of punch marks. It's flaky. Layers peel away.

Stone on top of steel, on top of wood, on top of water.

Peel away the layers. The wood has rusted. The steel has holes where nails have been. These holes can never be filled. They don't join up, not ever. Once the hole is there it's always there, somewhere, under the surface. The nail pushed the grain apart, forced itself into the wood. Sometimes the wood splits. Sometimes it opens smoothly. If it's hard wood, dry wood, then the nail needs to be hammered in. If the wood is soft, moist, fresh, then the nail slips in easily. This wood has many holes. It's been used for many things. It was once soft, smooth to the touch. Now it's hard. The years have dried it out. Rusty nails have toughened it up and stained it.

Coils and coils of skin. Wound, wiry, tight. That's the way of it. See the reflection, here.

Melting metal. Melting point. Heat up, red hot. Steel. Glow. Molten. Stroke the molten steel. Stroke the steel. She cups it in her hand. The wood catches fire, the wood burns, it ignites, and it too, flows.

Carbon mixes with the molten steel. Liquid scorches the wood. Steel inside the wood. It pours into the wood. The wood gives in. Peel off the skin. Peel off the layers. Get inside the steel. Get inside the wood. Stroke the wood. Open up the wood. Feel the grain. Feel it creak and groan like a sailing ship. The wood leans back and gives itself up. Smell the wood. Smell the dust. It's dry, but will catch fire in his hand.

The wood opens up and ignites.

Insolation

Lucy's eyes are different shades of green. The left eye's a little lighter coloured than the right, but maybe that's to do with the scratch. The left one has this small mark on the surface, like a scratch on glass. It's been there since she can remember. You'd hardly notice it if you were talking to her. It's a tiny line that runs across her left iris and pupil. She'd need to point it out to you. She'd have to say, here, look close. It's there, right across the centre. As she'd say that she'd pull down the skin just below her eye.

You move in close and look as she tilts back her head. You see the scratch that's been there since she can remember. You see it and say, oh yes, now I see. It's tiny, you say, there's hardly anything there. No one would notice that, you say, and when you're saying it you're really in close to her. She's a little shorter than you, and you're looking down into her left eye, then into the right. Her gaze is beyond you, up into the sky somewhere. You smell the lacquer on her hair. You smell her perfume. The air's rich and sweet, like cake mixture. You move in closer and see the lines below her eyes. You look at her neck, her jaw, then you follow the bone round to her ears then look back into her eyes. She blinks, focuses on you, smiles and straightens herself up. Her mouth parts and you notice the skin pull between her top and bottom lip. Her lips are dry and you look at her, then you step back and say, it's hardly a scratch. No one would notice, you say again. You say that and you've a burning sensation inside your mouth, a churning in your stomach.

Lucy notices the scratch. When she looks in a mirror she sees the scratch across her left eye. It's there, like a fault, but it's a scratch, that's all. It's just a tiny line. Maybe it's the way it catches the light that makes one eye look lighter than the other. Maybe. Maybe not.

You look at her you and you're lost for words. It's like you've absolutely nothing at all to say in the world.

Lucy. Tall, blonde, sun-tanned. That's me. Florrie calls me Luce, but she's just taking the piss.

Now he's got this big cloak type of thing. It's dusty and washed out, like an old sack or something. Damn thing makes him look like a tower from behind when he's got the hood up. You see him out there, even on a sunny day, and he's just standing there, still. If the wheat's long you don't see his legs, you just see that broad flat back of his poking up from all that yellow and green. You wonder what's going on in that mind of his.

Now I know the sky's in front of him, and it's grey. That's what it's like. It's grey and Ken stares a while then closes his eyes. The ground's wet. He licks his lips. They're salty. For a short while his eyes remain closed.

Columnar Structure

See the clouds there, high up?

I don't see anything, says Lucy.

You have to look close. Look up high, in between us and the stars. See that glow, that shine. It's like a veil. You only see them just after sunset. That's ice; fixed around meteor dust.

Yes, she says. Yes. Now I see.

I've got a lot to tell you, says Ken.

It's late, she says. I should be going.

Ken's head's on her stomach and she squeezes the back of his neck. It's like he's at sea. His eyes are closed and he's drifting. She strokes the back of his neck and says, you okay? He open his eyes.

As I said, he's on her stomach.

You've been asleep there for an hour or so, she says.

Can you not stay a while? He says that, then he looks up at her.

I'm sorry, she says and he moves up a touch onto her chest. He can hear her heart beat. He has an image of something smooth and red, of something small.

That poor kid who sat opposite me was like some vessel or shell. They tried to suck the insides out of him. I could have told them they could never do it. No. Not with him, anyhow.

I could tell you about the day I saw him out in that field when there was this real heavy hailstorm and the sky was like a sheet of aluminium, but you'd think I was just making it up or exaggerating.

Damn poor kid's in his forties and wears a sack over himself. He's not miles away from the rest of us. No. He sat there, on that damn stool and stared at those tiles in the palm of his hand. He knew I'd seen what happened. I'm sure he knew I'd seen.

Northern Lights

I don't want it to stop, says Lucy.

Then let's make a space clock and stop time. Everyone's made a space clock. You know, out in a field.

No. No, I've never heard of them.

Well let's do it. Let's go and stop time. I know just how it works.

We used to do it when we were young, me and Ray. We said we'd try to fool God into thinking it was a different time. We'd flatten out a circle in a field and lie there, me as the big hand, Ray as the small hand. We'd say it's four o'clock, God. And then we'd lay there, still. We'd think he'd make time stop if he saw our clock, that he'd think something had gone wrong. We'd think he'd look down at this field and see time from space.

The two of them lie down, heads touching. They've flattened out an area in the field. They flattened out the wheat and they lay down in their circle like hands on a clock. Him the big hand, she the small hand. They're lying with their heads in the centre, ear to ear. From above the clock reads six.

They look up at the stars, at the millions of stars in the sky. A little clock out in a field in the middle of nowhere. Two hands staring up; silent. A clock that's stopped, a clock that's decided to wait, to watch, to stop time. No more time. Wait. They're both lying in the stillness of the night.

I can tell you that Ken treats everything like it's delicate, breakable. Yet the skin on his hands is tough and thick. His eyes are dry.

I think, she says, I think the stars are going to fall out of the sky any minute. I think they're all going to drop, one by one, and land out here, in nowhere.

They can't fall, not while we're watching. Ray said that if you look away for a while, then when you look back, they might have moved. But if you stare at them they stay in the same place. So we don't close our eyes. We don't take our eyes off them. We don't move. We don't go anywhere. We just lie here. Head to head. Cheek to cheek.

Lucy and Ken, eh?

That's right. Lucy and Ken. Star watchers. Concentrate now. Don't let them move.

I wonder what we'd look like from up there, she says. Two tiny dots next to each other. Do you think it's worked?

Keep watching, says Ken.

The window's open a few inches and drops of rain are regularly spaced along the base of the frame. I've been watching for a while now. From this angle they have black bases but turn gradually lighter as they reach the wood. They're something like inverted bells and when they rock and shake in the wind the light catches them differently, but they don't make a sound, not that I can hear. After a while one of the drops grows larger. It swells up as more moisture runs down the glass. Then it reaches a critical point and drops free. I know if I look away for a while then they'll soon be gone. The sun's out now. It's warming up the frame, that glass and the walls of this room.

Wet Bulb Temperature

you were watching me
she says

he holds onto his book
         open at a page
and says
         maybe,
               but just out of one eye

only one eye
         she says
               and sighs
is that all

he waits for a moment
         thinks,
               then says
i'm blind in the other,
         i'll blind you
            she says as she pulls at his chest
            and tosses the book to the floor

not in my good one
         please
he says
         not in my good one

she laughs
         and says
               you're stupid
what do you mean
         he says
               you're just stupid
               you were born stupid

that's how it was
her naked
curled round his back
        her breath on his neck as she spoke

Maybe this is what it's like under the surface of the rest of the world. This is a world turned upside down, turned inside out. It's a world where hills have sunk and valleys have filled. A world that's been washed, laid out and ironed flat. It's a world that can't get any lower without drowning. Fields and fields and fields to the horizon and back. East and west, look both ways, spin on your heels, see the landscape become a disc, become a blur. Flatness that extends forever. A world that extends forever.

In Spring, when the storms arrive, the sky's lead grey. You can see the rain being dragged across the distance. Great clouds, darker than the rest of the sky. Light from behind shines over the fields. See the rain move. See the sky move. It's all over there, all in the distance, all on the horizon. You see it and you want to be over there, where it's pouring. You want that piece of the sky to head towards you, to soak you through but instead it moves sideways, on its low axis, like it's circling you .

This is the end. This is the graveyard of hills. This is the place where all the sand and silt and clay that's washed from the mountains ends up. You can't do anything but stand and stare. This is empty space; one way, or the other. Spin on your heels. Lose Spring, and see Summer, when the fields have turned yellow and the sky's sharp blue. Keep spinning, through rusty Autumn with its billowing white clouds and burning trees, and keep going, faster and faster, through Winter's dark earth and dull sky, spin through it all, all the colours you can remember, all mixing together, all blurring into blindingly bright white light.

Hygroscopic Nuclei

In Florrie's room there's a drip that comes in from the ceiling. There's a steel bucket positioned to catch the rusty water. Even if there's a drought the ceiling drips. Even in summer, when it's hot, when its not rained for days and days, when there's been nothing but blue skies and sunshine that ceiling still drips. They've tried to have it mended, but it's never worked. They've had builders and roofers and joiners up there, but the ceiling's always dripped. One guy said they needed a whole new roof, another said the gutters needed replacing. They came up with different solutions each time but the one thing that remained constant was that drip.

So now they've given up. Now they've decided to let the drip, drip. Florrie just needs to empty the bucket every now and then. She was going to do it last night, but then she forgot. She went to the window when Lucy hadn't come back. She went to see if she could see her over at the docks, or at the bridge. But it was dark, almost black, and she couldn't see a thing.

In the day, from Florrie's window, you can see where Ken lives. If you look over to the left, across the bridge, over to Old Goole, you can see Ken's house.

Now, the next morning, Florrie watches Lucy walk over to the bridge.

Water drips from the ceiling. She thinks about emptying the bucket, just as she's thought about it every day for the last week or so, then she looks back out of the window at Lucy.

Ken keeps his crackers in a tin box in the kitchen. He opens the box and lays the tin lid on the table. The silver reflects a patch of light onto the ceiling and he eats over the lid, like it's a plate. As he eats, crumbs drop onto the lid. The reflection on the ceiling looks like the sky on a Spring day when the sun's low and the blue turns to that bright silvery white that hurts your eyes. The crumbs make darker patches that look like clouds. Those clouds are crackers, and the sky's a reflection of light on the ceiling. Put the lid back on the tin and the sky and the clouds disappear.

Seems like the whole world's contained in a tin box in a kitchen in Goole.

Low Zonal Index Circulation

Ken's alone at the kitchen table. Each time he raises the spoon to his mouth he tilts his head forwards. The spoon touches his lips and he sucks in the hot soup. His lips part, fractionally, and he drinks the liquid by filtering it through his teeth. As the small hollow of the spoon is emptied he tilts his head backwards and swallows.

That's the way Ken eats. He eats slowly. He talks slowly. He does everything slowly.

The spoon returns to the bowl. He grasps the bread, tears off a piece then dips it into the clear soup. His head moves forwards and he meets the food as he raises it. He draws it into his mouth then swallows. His eyes close for a moment.

When the bowl is almost empty he wipes the sides with the remaining bread. Then he takes the bowl and the spoon to the sink. He washes the bowl in the cold water, places the bowl on the draining board then rinses the spoon. He places the spoon next to the knife and fork that's on the side. He's careful not to rattle them together as he places the spoon down.

Cellular Fragmentation

You know, says Ray. That cheese you've got is made up of millions and millions of tiny little pieces.

He raises his glass of Dandelion and Burdock to his lips and slurps the liquid down.

Ken's holding a lump of cheese in his hand. He's seven years old. He looks at the cheese then watches Ray gulp at his drink. Ray finishes, then bangs the glass down on the table. He lets out a huge sigh, wipes his mouth with his sleeve and smiles.

And this is the same, he says as he taps on the table. This wood's made up of millions of little things called atoms. Tiny things, they are. Like little grains of sand, all packed tight together.

Ken stares down at the table.

Shut up and let him eat, Ray's mother says.

They never touch, says Ray. These little atoms never touch each other no matter how hard you press. There's nothing ever touched anything else in the whole wide history of the universe.

Fifteen billion years of separation. Fifteen billion years of nothing touching anything else.

Some history that is.

The sky's big outside. The clouds over to the left there are glowing pink. In the distance, far behind them, the sky's light blue. Over that way, to the right, the clouds are blue-grey. The whole of the sky's drifting from right to left. It's windy. The trees out back of the garden are swaying. It's late October. Everything seems to be moving.

You know, I'd get images of Ken like that; images and sounds from his past. He would never tell me about those things. That's not the way he was. But I got to know a lot about him from that weather machine. I got to know a lot about Lucy, too.

This next part is Lucy. I remember it clearly. I remember it like it was yesterday. She's in the kitchen. If I close my eyes I can see her now. Clear as day, she is. Clear as day.

Cloud Base

I swear these boots will be the death of me. You wouldn't think they'd still hurt after all these years. Look at them, all ragged and scuffed. They've been heeled twice, but they still rub like anything. I keep meaning to throw them out, but then I don't. I keep meaning to do a lot of things.

I could live off this stuff, you know. Chicken soup for breakfast, chicken soup for dinner, chicken soup for tea. Soup with bread. Soup with chips. Soup and dumplings. Lovely.

I like standing here, stirring. I like watching the soup go round and round. I like the smell, the colour.

Look at it swirl and swirl.

Hear that? That's the upstairs window. It's Florrie's window. She'll be yabbering away to someone or other knowing her.

Florrie doesn't do anything in the kitchen; except talking and eating. She'll be down in a minute. She'll have smelled this soup and she'll be thinking, great, dinner time. This is her soup kitchen.

She can't get out of bed of a morning. She said, if we buy this place then you'll have to make the breakfasts. I said, well you have to tidy round and do the bedding and things. So that's how it is. Flo does the cleaning. I do the cooking. She hoovers and polishes. I make the food. She sorts the bedrooms. I sort the kitchen.

I can't stand fixing beds for strangers. Flo doesn't mind, but me? Not after my experiences.

But there you go. That's me and Flo.

I was round at Ken's just before. I'd gone round to say sorry for the other night. I didn't think I could do it before I went. I knocked on the door and thought I was just going to stand there, looking stupid, not being able to say anything. I couldn't sleep for thinking about what I'd done. I was going over and over the way he'd looked at me.

I should've guessed saying sorry wouldn't be easy. Anyhow, all I know is right now I want to make the best chicken soup I've ever made. I want it to be right.

So I'll stand here and stir and stir and stir till it's perfect. This is part of saying sorry.

There's Florrie's window again. She'll be down in a minute. I know
Florrie, I do.

If I keep my eyes closed I'm back at that machine. I'm out in the middle of wide open space and I'm hungry to listen to Ken and Lucy and Florrie. I'm fascinated, you see. Or at least I was. I knew these people, these characters from Goole, and I wanted to know what they said, what they did, what they wanted.

It's funny, really. There's me, wanting to create a shroud of mist or wanting to make the wind blow down from the north for a change, but what did I do? I used Ken, and listened in on Lucy and Florrie. It was easy. I'd got used to the controls. I just shifted the focus slightly, honed the antenna, and I had it; I had Florrie on the screen. This is Florrie. She's in her room; talking to herself.

Monsoon

You know what I've done, don't you? I just cut myself adrift. I've just shot myself out into space. It was a measly bucket of water, and a fraction of a second, that's all.

I saw him, Silo Man, coming this way. I couldn't believe it after what'd happened that night. I saw him, and then I twigged. He was coming here. I knew it. I knew he was coming here to meet Luce.

It's like I saw it all real clear and I thought no way. There's no way you're going to get my Lucy. So I watched him, and as he got over this way I opened the window and said, hey. I've something for you. You think she wanted you round here? Well I've a message for you. Lucy says swim in this, Moby.

He stopped still and looked up at me. I was holding the window with one hand and with the other held that silver bucket on the ledge.

I froze, you know. In that moment, I froze, solid. It was like everything in the whole world stood still.

I'm looking down at him. Ken's looking up at me. There's nothing else except the two of us, that open window, and that bucket. Christ knows why it's like this. The docks over the road are silent. The clouds aren't moving. The sky's still. Everything's stopped. Even the water over the road has turned grey. There's no sun. Everything's solid and lifeless. You wouldn't think anything would move again. You sort of hope it's stopped for good, but no. It's only temporary, like everything. The world stopped for a second or two. Everything stopped when the bucket was in balance. It could have gone either way. Sure it could. But then I tipped it and time starts again and there's nothing between us except water and collapsing distance.

And in that fraction of a moment as the water was leaving the bucket, in that tiny space of time when I knew couldn't do anything about it, as that rusty red water that had been collecting upstairs for god knows how long was leaving that bucket, I saw something of what Lucy saw. I'm sure of it. I'm sure. It was like a bolt of lightning or something. I looked up at the sky and thought, my god, what have I done?

Then boy did it hit him. Boy did it rain down on him. The whole heaven's opened up. I wouldn't have thought you could get so much water in one damn bucket.

But then it was too late. That water dropped like it'd been saved up just for that very day. It was like the water was going home, like it was being drawn to a magnet, like it had one place and one place only to go.

I'd seen him for years, over that side, over there. But he was always, over there, you know. Everyone knew about him. We all knew of him, but no one knew him, not really. He was just *That Guy*, The Weirdo, The Silo, The Tall One, Moby. You know what I mean.

Sure, we all knew of him all right. You couldn't not know of him, even from this side of the river. You could probably see him from the moon.

Then I took my hand off the window and it slid down shut.

It's not like a hole in his stomach. No. At first he thought of it being like a hole. But then, later, he'd thought that if it was a hole then maybe it could be filled again. He thought if it's like a hole in the ground then there's all that earth that's been removed and you could get some more earth and fill it in again. But it wasn't like that.

This. This thing. This is something that can't be refilled. There's nothing that can go into that hole.

Ken's memories are being torn apart, they're thinning out. It's like they're turning from solid to liquid to gas or something. They're getting more and more diffuse. All he has left is a few fragments, that's all.

Coriolis Force

Light scatters through the skylight over to the left. He stares for a moment, for a year, at the dust in the shaft. The dust rides up on a thermal, up to the glass. Ken touches the beads around his neck.

He lifts the latch and pushes the frame. The window opens and black dust falls into the hall. He looks at his hands; blackened from the dust and grime. Then he moves himself up to the slates and sits astride the crest of the roof.

It's quiet on the street. He leans back against the chimney, breathes deeply, and places his hands either side of himself, flat on the tiles. He positions his legs and when he feels balanced he relaxes.

The sky in the distance glows orange and red. The slates are warm. They're smooth, like well worn shoes. The gap between the bricks on the chimney is wide. The chimney pots are grimy, black. The lights have gone out on the docks and the cranes stand tall, like ladders in the sky. The river flows slowly in the dike.

He's on the roof of the house. Lucy's side saddle on a kitchen stool, cigarette in hand. But you know that.

Then maybe Ken's not on a roof top in Old Goole looking at the sunset. Maybe he's not across from the dike, across from the bridge, across from the docks. No. Maybe he's in New Mexico, in the desert, and he's on the back of a flour-coloured horse. They trot along. Red rocky mountains over to the left, stony ground underfoot, dust in the air. Ken licks the salt off his lips.

Then Ken blinks and he's not in some dry desert, or on a roof in Goole. No, he's in a wooden boat, out at sea. He's sitting in the middle of a long wooden rowing boat. The man at the front of the boat is holding a harpoon. Have you seen the whale? he says.

The man with the harpoon is wet, oily, greasy. Ken's rowing. He's pulling and pulling on the oars. Waves crash around the man at the stern. There's clouds, wind and rain all mixed in together. But Ken? Ken's in the desert.

Faster, shouts the man as he turns to look at Ken. The oars are in the sand, in the dust, in the dried-up river bed.

Ken's on a house, on the back of his house. He's on a horse and he's in a boat. Lucy's side saddle on a stool in the kitchen.

He's chasing himself, rowing after himself. He's helping the man with the harpoon chase the whale.

The black river dries and turns into a wadi. A small river bed filled with sand, gravel and stones.

Lucy's opposite Florrie. Her stool wobbles and then she's on the back of a horse. She's side saddle on the back of a flour-coloured horse. She wraps her arms around Ken's waist and buries her face into his back. The sky glows pink and bright.

I said this is a love story. But then maybe you didn't believe me.

You know what makes me think of Ken? I was out today, looking at some trees by the edge of that drainage ditch over there, out the back of the house. It's funny, really. I've been that way a thousand times and it only struck me today.

Along one side of the path there's the remnants of a hedgerow that's been torn to shreds. Saying that though, there's some thorn bushes, nettles, some sycamore and ash trees. You know, I'd never looked closely at the bark on ash trees before. Bark's bark, I thought. But, this morning, I stopped for a while and looked up close at that tree. It was there, at the edge of this ditch, leaning like it was about to topple over. Some parts of the trunk were thick, soft, crumbly. But, in between these there were parts that seemed like the tree was too big on the inside. It was like the skin was too tight, like it'd started to split and crack. It was like the skin had been outgrown.

I've been along that path a thousand times but today I felt like I was looking right at him. It felt like he was crumbling in front of me, like he was finally falling. Poor kid's just as weak as all of us; no matter how he seems.

Lapse Rates

Lucy opens the fridge door and puts the milk, cheese and butter inside. She turns, looks at Florrie, then flicks the switch on the kettle.

Florrie watches Lucy as she turns and rests against the sink. Lucy's staring out of the window. Her shoulders are hunched up, her head's tilted upwards. Maybe she's listening as the kettle rumbles. Maybe she's watching the sky move. Maybe her eyes are closed.

The kettle clicks off. Lucy raises a hand to her forehead and rubs her temples. Tea, she says and she lifts the kettle and pours the boiling water into the teapot. She takes two bags from the jar to her left and drops them into the water. Then she puts the lid on the teapot.

She walks over to where Florrie's sitting and she places the teapot down onto the table. Outside it's grey and overcast.

Flo and Lucy are opposite each other. Florrie's the one with both legs tucked under the stool. Lucy's side on, legs crossed at the ankles. The one on the left, Florrie, she has brown hair and dark lines on her forehead where there used to be eyebrows. She has thin, wrinkled lips and a mole on her right cheek, close to her nose. She's tanned, underweight. Her trousers are loose fitting. The skin on the soles of her feet is thick, callused. Her fingernails and her toenails are painted the same shade of light pink. Her nails are thick, grainy. Every now and then she touches the right hand corner of her mouth as she lets out a small cough. She holds a cigarette in her left hand. She curls her toes round the bar on the stool.

Now Lucy's up in front of Florrie. She's cleaning the yucca plant with kitchen roll and she's concentrating hard. She turns the pot one way, rubs a leaf, steps back and thinks a while. Then she moves close, rubs away again then turns the pot the other way. The leaves are shiny but the tips are brown, dry and crispy.

She curls one of the leaves and scratches at its underside.

This has that stuff on like the ivy, she says. Then she rubs away at the leaf again.

Flo takes a drink of tea and glances up at Lucy. Lucy's over at the sink now. She's washed her hands and is looking for a tea towel. She goes to the cooker and takes one from under the bills. She dries her hands then pushes the towel down in between Flo's back and the stool. Then she lifts one of the bills and looks at it. She's looking at the electricity bill and she's singing to herself. Flo can't make out the song and she wonders what Lucy's thinking about. She wonders whether she's paying any attention to the bill, whether she's thinking about the plant, about the weather or about anything at all. The soup's simmering on the cooker. It's the chicken soup Lucy made earlier.

They'd had chicken for the last three days. They'd had a Sunday dinner on Wednesday. A chicken leg each, roast potatoes, green beans, gravy. The next day they had the cold meat and chips. They sat round the table and picked away at the ribs and bones. Lucy took hold of the wishbone, held it between her fingers and offered it to Florrie. Make a wish, she said.

Flo wrapped her little finger round the bone. They looked at each other and Lucy closed her eyes. Do we have to close our eyes? said Florrie.

Lucy opened her eyes and said, Florrie, of course you have to close your eyes. You can't break a bone with your eyes open.

Then Florrie closed her eyes and said, have your other wishes come true?

That's not the point, this one might. Come on, make a wish.

They pulled, the bone snapped, and Florrie opened her eyes.

You got it, said Lucy. You've got the wish. It's your wish, she said.

Here, said Florrie. She held the broken bone out. You take it, Luce.

No, no, said Lucy. It's yours.

Should we've wished before breaking it? I thought maybe you do it after you break the bone so there's no waste, said Florrie.

Lucy smiled and said, it doesn't matter, Flo. It doesn't really matter. She's looking right at Florrie and she's smiling. So what did you wish for, Flo?

I thought you weren't supposed to say, she said.

Lucy goes all sad looking. Florrie smiles and says, do you really want to know? But Lucy shook her head and said, no, don't tell me. It doesn't work if you tell.

Florrie turns away and says, the plant looks good. She says it looks shiny, then she touches a leaf.

I hope this one lives, says Lucy.

Florrie says, do you mean the leaf or the plant and Lucy just sighs. It'll be okay, says Florrie. Just keep it watered.

Lucy stands up and goes over to the cooker. She takes the lid off the pan and stirs the soup. She's using a big metal spoon and it scrapes on the base. Big puffs of chicken-flavoured steam fill the air.

This soup's been ready for ages, she says. She raises the spoon to her mouth and tastes the liquid.

Do you want bread or toast?

Toast, says Florrie.

Lucy opens the bread bin, takes out some white bread and places it in the toaster.

It's bright out now, says Lucy.

Clouds of steam rise from the pan. The clouds smell of chicken. Chicken-flavoured clouds fill the air. Who knows, tonight it might rain chicken-flavoured rain.

Makes you wonder about that chicken. Sure, it's been boiled away but there must be some chicken in the air because I can smell it out here in these fields. Makes you wonder what it is that makes this chicken smell. I can tell it a mile off. It doesn't get drunk, or eaten. It doesn't just fade away into nothing. Sure, it gets thinner and thinner. Those little chicken-flavoured atoms evaporate off into the air and get further and further apart. That chicken smell gets weaker and weaker. Sure. The thing that makes the smell is always there. It goes out the window and floats round the streets, over the dike, and across the rooftops. It floats around, you breathe it in, you taste it, analyse it, lick your lips and exhale. It floats higher and higher. That tiniest bit of steam, that cloud you made in the kitchen, it doesn't just stay in the kitchen. No. It goes all over. It goes round the world. Someone inhales it in Scotland, in Norway, in Namibia. The whole sky's steaming with clouds of chicken-flavoured soup.

Dew Point

Florrie takes the silver foil from the inside of the packet of cigarettes. She peels off the paper backing and lays the foil on the table. It crackles as she open it out.

The foil's thin, but she's careful. As she listens to Lucy she rubs the small dimples on the foil with her nail. The foil becomes shinier. Lucy talks. Florrie listens. When Lucy's finished speaking Florrie looks up. The foil's smooth. The four corners curl upwards slightly and she presses them down onto the table top. The foil sticks to her fingers, but, using her nails, she manages to leave it flat on the surface of the table.

Florrie sniffs then coughs.

I've already told you about the pain in her side. It's a bad pain. I'd say there's something wrong with her. But she doesn't say that. She just rubs a finger in between her ribs and snatches for breath.

On the table there's a phone, an ash tray and a cup with no handle that's holding two pencils and a pen. Florrie takes one of the pencils from the cup and rolls the foil round the pencil. She slides the foil up and down the shaft of the pencil, then slips it off. The foil's like a tall silver tower standing up on the table.

I said it's coming bright now, Flo.

Florrie looks up from the magazine and says, I saw that Moby guy on his roof.

I saw him out my window, half an hour ago. I meant to tell you, Luce. He was on the roof of his house, just sitting all natural, like he did it every day, like he was on a horse or something.

There has to be somewhere at the average point of tidal range. This is it. The bridge at Old Goole is around that point. A big tide, a Spring tide, shifts water way past the bridge up to the far bend. A low tide, a neap tide, means water just about gets to the east turn in the river. A normal tide, an average tide, and the water stops right below the bridge. There has to be somewhere at that point. This is it. It's no big deal. It's below the bridge that leads from Old Goole to Goole.

I remember following Florrie from the house. I can't even walk past there any more. But back then, back then, I watched every step she took. I watched and listened to every thought she had.

There was Florrie; on the bridge. And there was me; watching and listening. Poor Florrie. This is her, going crazy.

Convection

Last night Ken uncovered Lucy. He peeled back her cellophane and she was there, open. It was the first time she'd been opened in years. I'd thrown a bucket of rusty water over him just so he didn't smell so good, but that didn't stop them. How can he be so clean in a dirty place like this? He's polished. He's bright, like a new pin. He's like some shining knight, or some beacon or something. He's like all things metal. He's like silver and stainless steel and factories and bridges. Well, what's the big deal? Lights go out. Lights don't burn forever. Things don't go on and on. Things go rusty. Not everything's made to be unwrapped. Everything ends up like this. This is black. This is empty. This is Goole.

Lucy said she'd been so long wrapped in plastic that she'd forgotten how the air smelled. She said she'd forgotten how to breathe. She said she almost suffocated when her wrapper was peeled away. She felt the sun on her face, felt the rain and wind. Then she stood up high on that roof and said she didn't realise the sky was so bright.

All this is after they'd met, you know. But I suppose we might never have met like this, me and Ken, if it wasn't for that steel bucket, that clean smell of perfume, and for Lucy.

Ken won't talk to me, not directly. He speaks to Lucy. That's how I hear him. Sure I hear him. But as I said, he never talks to me. He wouldn't do that. Not Ken. Not now. Now he leaves it for me to guess what he's like.

I tried talking to him; after a fashion. I tried out the window, when I had that bucket in my hand. But he just stared up at me. I suppose he might've said I had it coming. I laughed and tried to tell him the sky was turning red, like rust. I tried to tell him it's raining red rain from silver clouds, but he just stared at me with those cold eyes of his.

So I stand here on this bridge, salute him and say he's a horizon watcher. Yes sir. The clouds will stay on the horizon, he says. And that means the weather will remain the same. It'll stay the same for a while, he says. Then he nods and says, then it will change.

I didn't understand about horizon watching till I met Ken. But now I understand. Now *I* watch the horizon. But now there's no time anymore.

Now everything's empty.

I could see it coming, sure I could. The world slowed and slowed then ground to a halt. I saw it and tried to tell Lucy. Shit. Now she's not even wrapped in cellophane.

Maybe they've removed all the things that made this place what it should be and left us with this bone yard.

All this mud round here came from the mountains. This mud was once solid rock. It was granite or slate or limestone. It was a cliff or a jagged bluff. It was all up there, above the clouds. You'd think it wouldn't get rained on it was that high. But I know what it's like. It gets knocked down. The wind and the rain and the rivers and the ice and the snow and the heat and everything that can knock a mountain to pieces knocked them to pieces and now those mountains are just mud on the banks of this river. Those mountains are spread out flat over the fields out there and I'm in it up to my knees. It comes all the way down here and ends up as this. It ends up stuck to your shoe, or under your nails. It ends up over there, where they grow things. It's just dirt, that's all. It couldn't hack it as a mountain so it gave up. This is the soft stuff. This is the stuff that couldn't last. This is the stuff that couldn't even stand the weather.

I'm in the mud in Goole and I'm sinking.

Mountains. Sure. I know what happens to mountains.

Time's stopped. That's what Ken says. He says there's no time. There's no nothing, he says, not now. How come he knew so long before me? Now he looks at the horizon, shrugs his shoulders and says, that's everything. Makes me want to throw a hook over that horizon and drag it in.

You know, Ken says all of everything, all of everywhere, is happening at the same time. He says it's all there, over that way, or in some other place, anywhere, but it's not here. Not now. He looks at me and his face is silver-grey, like a rain cloud. From a distance, he says, there's no time or anything. From a big enough distance it's all the same, he says. From far enough away we're just a dot. From far enough away nothing happens. So Ken says.

Stand on the bridge. Look east or west. Nothing's new anymore.

So, the weather will change. Ken says it will. It will change, he says. But then the weather is always changing. Clouds are always forming and dispersing again. In between the two, he says, it rains.

But then he looks up and says clouds are just purses of water in the sky. He cups his big hands together and lowers them for me to see. In the cup of his hands is a pool of blue water. The sky's reflected on the surface. Lucy's in there, he says and I hold on to him and take a look.

Then he opens his hands and the water drops to the ground. So I look at him and say those clouds aren't purses in the sky, they're buckets and the water in the buckets is rotten. The buckets are full of rotten water that tastes like piss and lemons and batteries. The sky's filled with rust. That's why it's so deadly. That's why they put it so high up.

He just stood there and said you've never seen anything. That's when I looked up and the sun hurt my eyes and made them water. That's when I knew he'd met Lucy. I tried to stop them, but throwing that water over him was the best I could do. Now I cup my hands together and all there is in the palm of my hands is rust coloured water.

I'd laughed, you know, I'd laughed and said he could scrub himself clean. You'd think he wouldn't be shiny any more. You'd think after all of this time out in the rain and after everything that's happened, you'd think he would have lost some of his gloss. You'd think he'd be pitted and would need a scrub. But no. Not Ken. I'd tell you more, but as I said, he won't talk to me any more. I have to listen for him.

Ken's light, you know. You wouldn't think it to look at him. But he is. There's not an ounce of fat on him. He's big, but that's all. He's not heavy, like iron. If he was iron then he'd rust. If he was iron ore he'd be all flaky and rotten by now. His skin would be peeling and you'd be able to see under the surface to his weaker spots. He'd be like some rusty boat or some old oil drum. But no. Not him. Ken's some mix that doesn't go rusty. He's a thinner metal, a lighter metal, like an alloy. He's some mix up of metals. He's not like old nails and nuts and bolts. He's bright and silver and shiny and smooth. Nothing sticks to him, you see. Everything slips off him.

When I saw them together I had to look away. I thought I was going to be sick. I got the waterworks in my mouth and I thought if I turn away they won't see me. But then maybe no one would see me and that's what I was afraid of. I didn't want to be a cloud of dust. So at the end of everything I'm here. I'm like those clouds over there but I'm no purse of water. No. I'm grey and lifeless.

Now I can't even go over there. There's nothing for me over that way. I get halfway across the bridge and have to stop.

That stuff down there's not water, you know. It used to be water. When it fell on the mountains it was water. But this is no real river. This never used to be here a few hundred years ago. Sure, you've a real river coming in at one end, and it goes out into a river at the other, but this bit's all false. It's all invented. The river doesn't bend here, and that's not natural. You shouldn't get things like that. They should've put some curves in here and there. Look one way, look the other. It's all too stiff and straight.

I tell you, though, this bridge is no bridge. It's a brace. It's a bracket or some join or hinge or something. It's to hold that part of the world to this. Knock it down, I say. Get rid of this damn bridge. Let's watch the river get wider and wider. Let's watch that side float away.

I reckon this is just a crack. It's a crack that opened up a hundred years ago and they don't want us to know about it. That's what's happening all round here. All these dikes aren't dikes. All those drainage ditches aren't drainage ditches. That's just what they want us to believe. No. It's not what's really happening. What's really going on is this place is cracking up. It's drying out and it's shrinking. It's shrinking like mud does in the summer and it's leaving all these cracks around the place. Only they can't tell us that. They don't want us to know the world's falling to pieces. No. They say *they* dug the ditches and drains and dikes. Don't worry, they say, it's meant to be like this.

But I know what's going on. I know why they've built these bridges. Once it really splits open then we'll know about it. Then someone will have to pay. These bridges are braces between the old and the new. They're holding all these gaps together. But it doesn't fool me. I know what I'm standing on. I know what this is. I know concrete and iron and steel.

You know, Lucy's clock had started ticking again. She started moving and turning again. You could see it in her face. Funny thing is, you know, the funny thing is, is that she went out into that field to stop time, but that's when she started ticking again. The two of them, together, lying down in the grass and her clock went tick, tick, tick. I've not had a second go by in years. Then she goes up on that roof with him. So what if the view's good. Views aren't everything.

I'm just a few yards from the road, from the houses. It's a neap tide. We know these things in Goole. We know about Spring tides and neap tides.

I said she should get stilts so she can reach up to him. His damn legs are as long as me. They're like tubes. Besides, Lucy doesn't like heights. Why'd she want him to lift her all that way up there? She doesn't like open space. She's doesn't like grass and fields. It's filthy, all that stuff. It's just muck. She doesn't want to go out back there. What's she want to do that for?

She was really high up, you know. He had her in his arms. He was holding her waist and he lifted her straight up, like she didn't weigh anything at all, like she was just made of air and clouds. He raised his arms and then her feet were up there somewhere, somewhere they've never been before. I could see the two of them. I shouted for her to get down. I said she might fall, or he might drop her. But she just went up and up like she was never going to stop, like she was a rocket or something. I didn't know arms could be that long. How does anyone have arms like that? She just kept going and going and going and I thought that's it. Bye Lucy. I thought she's never coming back. I thought now she's been off the ground she's not coming down again. I shouted, just the same. I thought I'd warn her. But out there, out the back, in nowhere, a voice gets lost. Out there the wind catches what you say and it twists it around. My voice got picked up and was carried off by the wind or something. Then it came back. The wind got stronger and maybe it made what I'd said louder, because when it came back it wasn't like an echo. You don't get echoes out in flat space. No. It was louder than an echo. It was twisted and mixed up and it was thrown back at me. Get down, it was saying. You put her down. She'll fall.

That wind was hard, and got right inside me; under my skin. Doesn't matter how many clothes you wear when it's strong like that. It gets right

135

through to the marrow. I watched her up on that rooftop getting higher and higher and higher.

Absolute Zero

Then she fell.

When I was a kid my dad used to say the sea turns the same colour as the sky. He said when the sky's blue the sea's blue. The sea and the sky are in cahoots, he said. He said when the sky's cloudy the sea's cloudy. When the sky's clear, the sea's clear.

Sometimes, you know, I've seen the sea and it's been green. I've never seen a sky like that. I never said that to my dad. I've never seen a green sky like the colour of a green sea.

There was one time when this friend of mine was painting a picture of the sea and in his picture the sea was green and purple. The teacher was going round the class saying how good all the paintings were. She came to his, this friend of mine, and she said, the sea's not that colour. The sea's not green, she said. She laughed and the rest of the class laughed.

This friend of mine said he looked at her and said you must have never seen the sea. Then the class went quiet. The teacher looked at him in a funny way and asked him what made him think it was green and he said, because I've seen it. I know it's green. Everyone knows it's green, he said. He said that some days all you see, all round you, is the green sea. He said that the sky might be clear and blue, that there might be no more than a ripple on the surface of the water. But, he said, the colour's there. You look down and the green goes on and on and it gets darker and darker. It's bottomless, he said. And, if the wind gets up, the waves get bigger, then you get patches of purple and black. The black bits are the worst, he said, but mostly it's green. It's not always blue, like the sky, he said, and he looked right at her and shook his head. Sometimes, from the shore, it looks blue, you know. When you're standing on the beach, or on a hill, or on a cliff, and you look at the sea, it might look blue. But when you're out at sea, when you're on a boat, or when you stand there and look, he said, it's green. I've seen it.

Lucy's dying. She's on the pavement, staring up at the sky.
The sky's perfect, she says.

Mirages 2

I looked and could see she wasn't with me. Lucy stared up and said, Florrie. It's getting brighter. Look Florrie, she said. It's bright and blue up there. See the clouds and the sun? See how bright it all is? But it's like she was made of glass or china or something.

She's on the concrete, shattered from when she fell.

Why'd she want to go and knock lumps out of that concrete? Can she not see there's nothing beneath it? There's no blue under there. All the blue got mixed up with all the other bits and got lost. And now it's all mixed together and it's all grey and baked; hard. She was never going to get through it. I could see it, from here, from the river. But she can't, not now. No. Not now that she's had her feet in the air.

Then, when she was down on that pavement, she closed her eyes and didn't say anything else at all. She did that thing she does with her top lip, biting it, sucking it in, and she tilted her head and looked away from me. But she didn't say anything. I had hold of her hand, saying it's all right, Lucy. It's all right.

That was a long time ago. That was before I sank into this mud, before Lucy was unwrapped, before Ken stood up on that roof. It was before Lucy was sprawled out like some ballerina.

Sure, she's seen ditches. She's seen fields growing wheat and barley. She's seen water in the dike flowing one way, then the other. But she's never even seen a rise in the landscape. She's only been as high as that rooftop in her whole life. But so what. Hills don't mean much. Hills aren't everything. I don't need hills. Plenty of people have seen hills. Not too many have had an eye full of emptiness. Not too many have seen all this. No. You go a long way to find these places. You scratch and scratch before you find such emptiness. But I've seen it. I've seen emptiness all my life. You want to know about this place? You want to know flat places or flat spaces? I could tell you some things. I could tell you some things all right.

I've seen flat. I've seen flat with a flat sky with flat colours and flat everything.

Ken and Lucy. Boy, Ken and Lucy. Now they've seen some things. They saw a cloud that was like a big anvil in the sky, and maybe you've not seen that. Sometimes you need it to be perfectly flat, just so you get a clear view. Makes it sound like all sorts of crazy things happened out there on that flat bit of land. That's what flat can do. Flat can paint a picture in the sky bigger than any painting ever painted, bigger than all the paintings in the world put together and timesed by ten. And Ken did it. He warmed up the ground and made a big anvil-shaped cloud in the sky.

Concrete and metal and mud and grass. Make them higher I said. Don't let the river overflow. Don't let me see the mud and the silt and the clay. I don't want to see the river when it's in flood or when it's dried up. I say divert it. Move it somewhere else. We don't need all these rivers. Fill it with concrete and make a road. We don't need more of them boats. They're too quiet. You can't trust them. You don't know they're there till you look round and there's this thing like some huge hotel that's floating past. They're too big, those boats. They're too white. They move too slowly. They block out the sun. They make you feel sick because they're so big and move so slow. You think it's the ground that's moving beneath you, but then you look and you know it's the ship that's going along the river, right next to the road. You can shout at the captain from here. You can see the time on that copper clock inside the cabin. You can see the men on the decks smile. They're doing things, working, washing, tying ropes. They're on a floating world and they don't see me at the side of the river. It's just there, feet away. They just float quietly along.

So drain it all. Get rid of this river. Build the embankments higher. I don't want to see the river again. I don't want to see that black water flow by. It's too deadly. I don't like water. There's too much of it. It's too wide. And it's not clean. It's never clean is that river water.

I know Lucy. I've known Lucy a long time, since we were young. We used to sit together at school. I've known Lucy all my life. Me and Lucy, we're like this, like two peas in a pod.

She wasn't supposed to meet Ken. She's not seen anything of the world in so long now. This is it, she said. It's all here, wrapped up, suffocating. Then she looked at me and said the world stopped years ago, didn't it Flo?

He was on that roof. That big guy was on the roof of his house and Lucy went up there with him. He lifted her up into the air and now look at her. Now she's dead on the pavement.

That old windmill out back there is like Lucy. It's got no sails, you see. Those sails have long since gone. The insides have gone, too. The workings don't work any more. The sails don't sail, the cogs don't cog. It's a shell. It's a casing that once contained moveable parts. Once, it blew with the wind. It creaked and groaned. It turned. It had life.

All those mechanisms; the stones, the shafts, the gears, well none of them can turn any more. It's lungs don't operate. Now, it can't use the wind. It can't draw breath. The insides are no use. The insides can't do what they're supposed to do. They can't grind anything to dust.

Lucy's a sail-less windmill. Her insides don't work. It's like she's been crushed. Maybe she's like flour. She's just a pile on the floor.

Ken reaches down and sweeps the flour into the palm of his hands.

Aurora

Sure. Ken knows he can't just stand up there and watch forever. Ken's seen the blacksmith's close. He's seen the sails disappear from the windmill. He's seen the fields stripped bare. He's seen great anvil-shaped clouds grow in the distance. And now Lucy's curled up. She's asleep on the pavement. She's as quiet and as soft as flour.

I'm still out here in these fields. I've been here sixty years now, and I'm still amazed. Let me tell you.

From where I'm standing you can see maybe twenty miles in each direction. I say twenty, but it could be more; it's just a guess. Out in front, or behind me, all around, the land's flat. I mean real flat. I saw a map once and there wasn't a single contour marked. This place is just a metre or so above sea level. It's so flat it sometimes makes it seem as though the ground curves, like it's rising up to the horizon. It's an illusion, I know, because when I'm over there, miles and miles out that way, when I'm over here, or back there, or over that place, it's exactly the same. You get the feeling there's a gentle slope as you look into the distance.

This time of the year the fields have started to turn green. They were brown only a few weeks ago. But now they're green with shoots of winter wheat. The green's hidden the lines, the plough lines, in the fields. A couple of weeks ago you'd be out here and your eye would be pulled one way or the other. The field over that way had furrows running north to south. That field out that way had them going east to west. You'd look over at the horizon and find your gaze drawn one way or the other.

But now the winter wheat's on its way those lines have been lost. Sure, there's still some pattern. The fields are still ordered. The wheat follows the furrows but the lines aren't as sharp. You can overlook them. Sometimes I think it's like they were never there. Now you can gaze over at the horizon without distractions.

I can stare over that way all day. It's strange, but when I moved here I didn't want flatness; not real flatness. I always wanted hills. I wanted valleys, and vantage points and crags and outcrops of rock. I wanted roughness. I wanted things to look at, things to fill up the view, things to block space. I wanted to see bare rocks poking up through the ground. I wanted to see places with grit and moss and stone.

But here, you know, here, there's none of that. You can't see the tiniest of hills from this place. It's like hills don't exist. It's like valleys don't exist. Everything's even. Everything's smooth. Everything's level and laid out. It's like there's nothing between you and the rest of the world. It's big, consuming, untouchable. This place is too flat to be part of anything. It's like the world exists over that way, or over there. Round here it's like everything exists some place else.

I'd thought about seeing it all from above. I wanted to see myself, see the fields, see the flatness. I wanted to see myself surrounded by a nothing landscape. I wanted to see this empty circle with a dot in the middle. From above, if you could get it all in, then it might make sense. It might be something you could look at and say, yes, now I see what it's like. I see it this way, or that way. From here, from above, I can get all that space under control. I can get it all in a single frame. I can understand.

From down here though, it's different. From down here it's big. It's big and out of reach. The view's unstoppable. So you need to get taller, see further, see more clearly. Climb onto some roof and you'll see to the end, to some hill, or valley or something that catches your eye.

It's funny, you know, but I'm frightened of open space. I see it though and want to stop and stare. It's the idea of emptiness. You don't get many places like this. You've got to appreciate them when you see them. Mountains, and rivers, and valleys, sure, they're all over. You don't need to travel far to see some rise in the landscape. But perfect flatness. Big wide open fields of nothing. Huge skies and iron grey clouds. You don't get many places like that. When you find one you've got to stop. When you find one you've got to try to take it in.

When Ken was a kid he'd take out the dominoes and clatter them around on the kitchen table. He'd place his big hands over them and he'd smile and swish them round and round. Then, one by one, he'd turn them over and join them together. Sixes, fives, fours, threes, twos, ones and blanks. He'd lay them in perfect straight lines. Then he'd turn them over again and swish them round and round.

It's a while now since we played. Boy could we play dominoes.

Stability

They've put a statue of Ken out the back, out there in the fields. It's a steel statue. The colour changes every second of the day. In the morning it's cold and dark and as green and as blue as ice. By the afternoon it's red and yellow and silver. Later in the day it's deep bronze. It depends. I say those colours but it's been different every time I've been. I saw him once, you know, and everything about him was black and purple, like he'd been bruised. Another time I went and it was like he was on fire. It was like he was about to explode or something.

Last time I was there I placed my hand on his arm. The arm was thick and cold. The statue didn't move. For some reason I expected it to. I expected him to acknowledge me. I thought I might feel a muscle move or some blood flow. I thought he might move his lips, or blink an eye. But he didn't budge. He just looked dead ahead.

He's got a wide, flat forehead. I remember not realising how big he was. From a distance, when you walk up to him, you look and don't realise how tall he is. You can't drive there. He's so far out into that flat space that you have to leave your car at the peat works and walk for an hour before you see him. And when you do see him over there in the distance he's just like a tiny speck. You think he's a small tree or something. Then you get closer and closer and it's not until you're right up to him that you realise how big he is.

Sure, I could just about touch his shoulders. His shoulders were big and solid and level. I never saw him slouch. Ken never slouched. Even when he sat in the kitchen, at the table, he sat with his back straight. His body's balanced. It makes him look awkward. It makes his movements seem unusual, difficult. But that's the thing, you see. He's more efficient than me. He can walk and sit down and stand up straight and tie his shoelaces and do anything without putting pressure on his back or his muscles. He's never pulled a muscle in his whole life.

I went round to the front and looked up at him. His eyes were bright and silver. They were fixed on some spot beyond me. There was no way on earth he was taking his eyes off the distance. He couldn't.

So I turned round and looked towards the horizon. You could see for miles from where we stood.

146

It was a clear day. A bright day, and Ken gleamed in the sun. I wondered what he was looking at. I wondered about the clouds, about the colour of the sky. I wondered about the long grass, about Lucy, about the river, about Florrie. We both looked south.

I wondered if Ken was seeing the same as me. A small white cloud drifted from right to left in the far distance and I watched it for a while, though I'm not sure for how long. The air was thick and warm. I thought maybe looking south would make some sense.

Then, I blinked, and it'd started to rain over there, miles away. I turned round and Ken wasn't with me. I was on the dockside looking at a container ship. It had the name ZANTOS written on the stern. All the buildings were grey, and I couldn't see the horizon any more. All I could see were steel constructions in front of me. People were working. The ship was being unloaded. It had tonnes and tonnes of food in its holds. The grain was yellow and brown, like dried mustard. There was this crane to the side of the ship. The crane lowered its jaws into the ship. When they emerged and rose, grain and dust fell from between its teeth. It swung over to the truck parked on the dockside and when above, the steel jaws opened. It was like that crane was eating the ship. The ship was getting lighter. You could see it getting higher in the water. The bottom half of the ship was red, the top, blue. I wondered if the ship would float off into the air. The air was dusty and it made me cough. Later I had crap in my nose when I blew it. I looked at the tissue and it was yellow and brown. I thought my insides might have changed to the colour of dust, wheat and tobacco.

That's when Lucy appeared. I saw the colour of dust, of mustard, of tobacco, of smoke, of all those things, and when I looked again Lucy was standing there. She was right in front of me; smiling. Her teeth were stained. She had yellow and brown marks around her gums.

I said, Lucy, you have a nice smile, and she blinked and her smile broadened.

Soon be dead, she said and she laughed a big loud laugh.

Sure, this place is big all right. I've hardly got the space here to tell you about it.

Maybe if you could get up there somewhere it'd all make sense. If you could get up in the sky and look down you'd see this big wide flat open space made up of all these pieces. You'd see the water that circles us all.

There's the Ouse over that way, to the east, the Trent that way, to the west. The Humber's to the north and to the south's the Keadby and Stainforth Canal.

All of this is history. A pity, really. It's a pity this history's like it is. Or maybe it isn't. Who knows? But reading this is like looking back in time. It's a reconstruction. This is what's gone. The stuff right at the end though, further on than this, well that happened a while ago. That happened years ago.

Even the rocks buried some place down beneath us surface at some point. It just takes time, I suppose, and maybe a few cold nights. It'll just take a million years or so, that's all. Sure, things get buried. Dust and dirt and sand and silt and gravel cover things up. But it doesn't cover things forever. No. It hasn't covered over Ken and Lucy and Florrie. Not yet, anyhow.

Cumulo-nimbus Revisited

Did I tell you that all that material from the dike was smeared over the earth before Old Goole was built? The engineers wanted to raise the level of the land, to reduce the risk of flooding. So they dug the dike real deep. They cut it straight. It's about half a mile either way before it bends, and all the mud and silt and sand and clay is now buried under Old Goole.

That used to be marshland, over this side. It used to be an island. From the Ouse, to the Trent. From the Don to the Stainforth and Keadby Canal, that area would have been an island. Naturally, rivers flood, you see. It used to flood every year. It rains up in the hills and water overflows its banks and floods the floodplain. That's why the land's so brown. That's why it's so flat.

Those engineers knew about the river. They knew what it did. They knew it'd flood. So they dug pits out the back of the houses. Now though, the land's been drained. Now, the trees have disappeared and the fields have got bigger and bigger. Now, you can't help but look off to someplace else.

Tell someone about the weather, the sky, about your day, about yesterday. Paint a picture. Fit the pieces together. See things unfold and appear. Watch as everything falls into place.

That sky's not just a blue sky. That cloud's not just a white cloud. That cloud over there in the distance, the one just above the horizon, that long thin one, there's never been another in all of history. So I gaze into the distance and say, look at that cloud. I say stupid things like it's a hot sunny day and the sky's blue. I say all sorts of stuff like that to myself. There's too much in a sunny day, in a breeze, in a rainstorm. Sure, there's too much to tell you about.

There's a tree just out the window from here. It's late, it's dark, but I can see the tree, black against a violet and blue sky. The tree's swaying in the wind. It's a tall thin tree; a cypress tree. The sun set about an hour ago but there's still some light around. I held my grandson up at the window. He's nearly two weeks old. He's fascinated by light. He'd only stop crying when he was upright, near the glass. The poor kid goes cross-eyed when I look at him. He stared out towards where the sky was slightly lighter. I know he doesn't know what clouds are, or what a sunset is, or even what colour is, but he stared and his face lit up. It's like the sky made him drunk. He can't generalise about it all like we can. He can't write words and sentences; not yet, anyhow.

I suppose I can't say for sure that he was smiling, but it looked something like a smile on his face.

This afternoon I was driving back to Old Goole. It'd been hot and sunny for the last few days but today the weather changed. Today the winds came from the north, so it was much cooler. On the road from Swinefleet I looked over towards the peat works. The sky over in the distance was a liquid mix of grey, silver and white. Directly in front of me, beyond the fields, the sky was wet looking. I'm sure that's where the rain was. That was the darkest part. To the right of that patch the sky was lighter where the sun was breaking through. To the other side, towards the river, the sky gradually turned to white then to grey again.

The fields in this part of the country are big. There's hardly a bush or a tree separating mile after mile of farmland. Over in the distance there's some oil seed rape. Against the grey of the sky the yellow field is really bright. To the left of the rape is green wheat. In front of that is barley. Sure, this place is bursting with colour.

It's raining now. It's been raining most of the day. The rain sounds light from here, but I know it's heavy. It's tapping on the bay window, on the glass and on the roof, but I know outside it's really pouring.

Someone once told me a typical cloud lasts for just twenty minutes. Twenty minutes. Can you believe that? I'm not sure. I've been here an hour or more and it's like nothing at all has moved.

I told you before that if the atmosphere was cooled far enough it'd turn to liquid, then to solid. It makes sense, I suppose. Cool water and it solidifies; it freezes. Warm it, it thaws, then boils and lets off steam. The whole pan might just boil away and all that water ends up up there somewhere.

The big difference with the atmosphere is that oxygen, and hydrogen, and helium and the other gases, have very low boiling points. Water boils at a hundred degrees Celsius. But oxygen? That boils at minus one hundred and eighty three degrees Celsius. That's a low boiling point for sure. If it's cooled further than that it could become solid. So, the atmosphere, this atmosphere, this layer of gases we breathe, this atmosphere that forms clouds and rains down on us, this atmosphere with blue skies and thunderstorms and great anvil-shaped clouds; it's just melted solid. It's just boiled up air. We don't think of it as boiling away up there. But it is; believe me.

It's just started to rain again. It's amazing, really. Sometimes you're sure it's not going to rain. It doesn't smell or feel like rain. Sometimes you can't even see a cloud in the sky. But that sky tricks you. You're out there in flat, empty space, and you feel the rain on your face. You look up and wonder where it's all coming from. Maybe there's someone, somewhere, up there with some steel bucket and they're laughing at you as you squint and look up into the air.

The highest clouds I've seen are called noctilucent clouds. They're some forty miles up in the stratosphere. The stratosphere's the layer that's above the troposphere. The troposphere, the lowest layer in the atmosphere, is the zone that contains all our weather. It's the zone with most of the gases and water and dust and pollution. Just about all the clouds we see are in the troposphere. Even the tallest clouds, the cumulo-nimbus clouds are contained in the troposphere. Sometimes they stretch right up to the boundary between the two layers then spread out like two arms. But those noctilucent clouds, they're way up in the stratosphere. You can see them at night. They're fine clouds. They're high clouds. They're made of ice crystals and they glitter like diamonds.

So, there it is. All there's left is the landscape. All there's left to tell you about is the sky and the clouds and the river and the fields and the bridge. It's pretty simple, after all.

There's a man who's alone like a giant. Giants are always alone in the world.

Evaporation

I've already told you what we're doing. We're out in this field and we're playing dominoes. Ken's in that old black suit of his. His face is white and round and I look at him awhile.

He's not normally so pale, poor kid. He had to help me out here. I pretended I could hardly walk. Hell, I don't even deserve his arm.

I wouldn't have believed it, you know. Ken doing all those things. It's like there was some freak storm or something. It's like he went crazy. He was even dancing with Lucy in that old house of his. Now there's something.

Seems like bad luck's been raining down on him since the day he was born.

So I look over at him again as he shuffles those dominoes round on the table. He's got big hands. They're real big and he's staring down at those tiles as they clatter and clatter around. We're way out here, out back, in this wide open space. Old Goole's back that way, a million miles behind us, but I don't want to look. Neither of us wants to look.

Go on then, I say. Pick it up then. I told you, we should call you double six. They may as well have glass backs, these dominoes.

It's the grey round here that really does it. Sure, the green helps, but it's that silver sky that's edging round the horizon that makes your stomach churn. I haven't met anyone who can just look and say, what was it you wanted to show me? No. There's no one alive that can't be swallowed up by it. I know. I was swallowed up a long time ago.

But then I've been looking over that way, since I can remember. You think it's empty space, but it's not really so empty. No. That space makes me smile inside it's that full. That space between you and the horizon is bursting. It's waiting to draw you in, and once you're in there, that's it, it's got you. There's no mountain anywhere in the world going to get you back from there. Space is space is space and this is space. Space between you and that horizon; miles one way, miles the other.

Overcast

We moved our table
further out into the fields
to play our dominoes

because now, his name's
not just Big or Moby, it's
That Guy,
the one who pushed her
or threw her
or dropped her

that poor woman
should have known better
should not have let him lift her
off the ground

so now they say
he did it, he's the one,
him, the tall one,
the one who let her go

so we moved our
table a little further out,
away from the road
and the footpath

not that we
could hear
anyhow,
but Florrie
saw what happened

and she said
it wasn't him
no,
she said,
Lucy slipped and fell

he lifted her
up to the clouds
but then she slipped
when he gently placed her
down

she turned to look
when I shouted,
and she smiled
and went to wave,
like she does,but she clattered
over that roof

then everything
went silent
whilst she was in the air
descending
like a fog

and with the crack
and thud
of a breakable mallet on stone
she turned
to mist

Aspect

I'd almost finished this last night. It seems strange to be able to say that, but I did. I'd spent the past few months thinking about what happened, then, last night, I had an idea for an ending. It went something like this:

From the window of this space rocket you can see the earth. The window's not much larger than my face and it's round, like my face. Look down and you can watch the towns and cities get smaller and smaller. All those lights merge into one until there's just a tiny spot of light. You can't really see that much, I suppose. It's a pity, really. I'd kind of like the rocket to stop moving so I could just stand here and watch, but now that white dot of light's getting dimmer and dimmer and all around it's getting blacker.

Other Titles From Route - Fiction

Very Acme
Adrian Wilson
ISBN: 1 901927 12 1 £6.95

New Nomad, nappy expert, small town man and ultimately a hologram – these are the life roles of Adrian Wilson, hero and author of this book, which when he began writing it, was to become the world's first novel about two and a half streets. He figured that all you ever needed to know could be discovered within a square mile of his room, an easy claim to make by a man who's family hadn't moved an inch in nearly seven centuries.

All this changes when a new job sends him all around the world, stories of Slaughter and the Dogs and Acme Terrace give way to Procter and Gamble and the Russian Mafia. He starts feeling nostalgic for the beginning of the book before he gets to the end.

Very Acme is two books within one, it is about small town life in the global age and trying to keep a sense of identity in a world of multi-corporations and information overload.

Like A Dog To Its Vomit
Daithidh MacEochaidh
ISBN: 1 901927 07 5 £6.95

Somewhere between the text, the intertext and the testosterone find Ron Smith, illiterate book lover, philosopher of non-thought and the head honcho's left-arm man. Watch Ron as he oversees the begging franchise on Gunnarsgate, shares a room with a mouse of the Lacota Sioux and makes love to Tracy back from the dead and still eager to get into his dungarees. There's a virgin giving birth under the stairs, putsch at the taxi rank and Kali, Goddess of Death, is calling. Only Arturo can sort it, but Arturo is travelling. In part two find out how to live in a sock and select sweets from a shop that time forgot and meet a no-holds barred state registered girlfriend. In part three, an author promises truth, but the author is dead - isn't she?

In this complex, stylish and downright dirty novel, Daithidh MacEochaidh belts through underclass underachieving, postponed-modern sacrilege and the more pungent bodily orifices.

Crazy Horse
Susan Everett
ISBN 1 901927 06 7 £6.95

Jenny Barker, like many young women, has a few problems. She is trying to get on with her life, but it isn't easy. She was once buried underneath the sand and it had stopped her growing up, plus she had killed the milkman. Her beloved horse has been stolen while the vicious *Savager* is on the loose cutting up animals in fields. She's neither doing well in college nor in love and fears she may die a virgin.

Crazy Horse is a wacky ride.

Other Titles From Route - Poetry

Half a Pint of Tristram Shandy
Jo Pearson, Daithidh MacEochaidh, Peter Knaggs
ISBN 1 901927 15 6 £6.95
A three-in-one peotry collection from the best in young poets. Between the leaves of this book lies the mad boundless energy of the globe cracking-up under our very noses; it is a world which is harnessed in images of jazz, sex, drugs, aliens, abuse; in effective colloquial language and manic syntax; but the themes are always treated with gravity, unsettling candour and humour.

I Am
Michelle Scally-Clarke
ISBN 1 901927 08 3 £10 Including free CD
At thirty years old, Michelle is the same age as the mother who gave her up into care as a baby. In the quest to find her birth parents, her roots and her own identity, this book traces the journey from care, to adoption, to motherhood, to performer. Using the fragments of her own memory, her poetry and extracts from her adoption files, Michelle rebuilds the picture of 'self' that allows her to transcend adversity and move forward to become the woman she was born to be.
You can hear the beat and song of Michelle Scally-Clarke on the CD that accompanies this book and, on the inside pages, read the story that is the source of that song.

Moveable Type
Rommi Smith
ISBN 1 901927 11 3 £10 Including free CD
It is the theme of discovery that is at the heart of *Moveable Type*. Rommi Smith takes the reader on a journey through identity, language and memory, via England and America, with sharp observation, wit and wry comment en route. The insights and revelations invite us not only to look beneath the surface of the places we live in, but also ourselves.
Moveable Type and its accompanying CD offer the reader the opportunity to listen or read, read and listen. Either way, you are witnessing a sound that is uniquely Rommi Smith.